FIRE ON THE MOUNTAIN

Anne Bullard

A KISMET® Romance

METEOR PUBLISHING CORPORATION
Bensalem, Pennsylvania

First Printing July 1993.

ISBN: 1-56597-072-1

Printed in the United States of America.

This book is dedicated in loving memory to my Mom and Dad. Their support and encouragement will be missed.

ANNE BULLARD

Anne Bullard lives in Virginia with her husband, Bill, and their two Golden Retrievers. She has two grown children, and three wonderful grandsons, who are the center of her life. Her love of history started her on a writing career. Under the pseudonym, Casey Stuart, she has written eleven historical romances and has won the Romantic Times Award for best Civil War Historical. This is her second contemporary, which she says she enjoys writing because she can use some of the interesting places she and her family have visited. Jackson Hole, Wyoming, was one of her favorite places, and she hopes all the wonderful friends they made while there will enjoy this story.

Other books by Anne Bullard:

No. 15 *A MATTER OF TIME*

ONE

MAY

Cody Jones stared unseeing out the window of the busy Houston airport. He was waiting for his flight to take him home to Jackson Hole, Wyoming, after spending two weeks in a Houston hospital. Home, but for how long? he wondered, a sick, empty feeling washing over him. The doctors, some of the best in the country, diagnosed his illness as an inoperable brain tumor, and at best gave him six months to live. Six months to do everything he hadn't done in his forty-seven years.

He closed his green eyes and pulled his cowboy hat low over his forehead. God, if he'd only known things would come to such an abrupt end. What would he have done? Bought that black stallion last spring, traveled more? Well, he did still have time to fix that cracked window in Cabin 3, and mend the fence on the corral. He clenched his fist, realizing how unimportant those things suddenly seemed. Hell, who was he kidding? There was only one thing that he regretted . . . one thing that suddenly seemed important. He had a daughter he didn't know. A daughter who was twenty-one, a year older than her mother had been when they had married after a whirlwind courtship, and he didn't even know what she looked like.

He thought of his ex-wife, Emily, and wondered if his daughter looked like her beautiful mother. Strange, he had spent years trying not to think of the statuesque beauty he had met while working at a dude ranch in Arizona. Now he was trying to remember every detail, hoping it would give him some insight as to what his daughter looked like.

He should hate Emily, and he had tried, but as time passed, he had realized their marriage had been sabotaged by one of the best. They'd never stood a chance against her manipulating mother, Agatha Van Payton, the matriarch of the family. They both knew her mother was against the marriage, but they were madly in love and were sure they could overcome every obstacle that stood in their way. Cody snorted under his breath. Yeah, every obstacle, but an overbearing, shrewd mother who was determined to have her own way. Better men than he had tried to stand up to the old lady and lost. At least he'd left with some pride intact, and he'd had his ranch in Wyoming to return to when the marriage broke up.

The Van Paytons had quickly put him out of their minds, not even bothering to inform him that Emily was expecting. His daughter was two years old before he even learned of her existence, and that was by chance. He'd run into a couple on a skiing trip whom he had known while in San Francisco, and they just happened to mention what an adorable daughter he had. He immediately headed for San Francisco, but the old lady did everything she could to prevent him from seeing his daughter, Charlene, or his ex-wife, and she had won. After two visits, it became obvious that the traumatic scenes were doing more harm to his daughter than good. Always present was Agatha Van Payton, a nanny, and a lawyer, and the visits were only allowed in the most austere surroundings. On top of the awkward circumstances, each trip to San Francisco was costing him money he didn't have.

He had tried for years to get them to let Charlene come to Wyoming to spend summers with him, but he had finally come to the conclusion that it would be better for everyone if he just faded out of the picture and pretended his marriage to Emily Van Payton had never taken place. And now he was going to his grave not having seen his daughter in nearly nineteen years.

"Flight 218 to Jackson Hole is now boarding at Gate 23" came a voice over the loud speaker.

Cody picked up his bag and started toward the gate, then he stopped. What the hell was he doing? He probably would never see his daughter if he boarded this plane back to Jackson Hole.

"Sir, your ticket . . ." the flight attendant urged as he blocked other passengers waiting to board.

"I've changed my mind. Where can I find out what airline has the next flight to San Francisco?"

"There's a ticket agent next to Gate 19, sir, but are you sure you want to do that? This is the last flight to Jackson Hole today."

"I've never been surer of anything in my life."

* * *

Several hours later Cody sat in a rental car across the street from the opulent Van Payton mansion. He went over what he was going to say to Emily and his daughter for the hundredth time. He didn't want them to know about his illness, but what should he say, that he was in the neighborhood and decided to drop by? Hell, what difference did it make what he said, he thought as he climbed from the T-bird and crossed the street. After nineteen years they'd probably be so stunned to see him that they wouldn't hear a word he said anyway.

Cody was surprised when the door opened, and Higgins, the same butler who had been there when he was married to Emily, greeted him. The old man must be as old as Methuselah, he thought with a grin on his handsome face. "Hello, Higgins."

The old man's withered face lit up. "Mr. Jones! By George, it's good to see you, sir. I often wondered what became of you."

"That's very nice to hear, Higgins. I'm glad someone around here has thought about me."

The old man smiled. "You were like a breath of fresh air around this old mausoleum."

Cody chuckled. "Things a little dull around here, eh?"

"Come in, sir, come in. What are you doing here after all these years?"

"I came to see Emily. I need to talk to her."

"Oh, sir, I'm so sorry. Miss Emily left this morning for Paris. She'll be gone at least three weeks."

"Damn, I'm sorry to hear that," Cody said, feeling as if the wind had been knocked out of him. "I really needed to talk to her."

"I can give you a number where she can be reached, sir," Higgins volunteered.

"Thanks, Higgins, but I need to do this in person. Tell me, did her mother go with her?" he asked, thinking he'd just have to do battle with the old woman again.

"Oh, sir, you didn't know . . ."

"Didn't know what?"

"Mrs. Agatha Van Payton died a few months ago, sir. She was two days short of her ninetieth birthday."

"I didn't know," Cody said. "I'll warrant she'll be a match for the devil."

Higgins laughed. "I imagine she will, sir. She was still ruling the Van Payton Enterprises with an iron hand until her dying day." Higgins glanced around to be sure he wasn't heard. "I can tell you it certainly has been peaceful around here without her—except for Miss Charlene's escapades. Come in and sit down, sir. I'll have Miss Simms make a pot of coffee for you. Do you still take it black?"

"I do, but I don't want to put you to any trouble, Higgins. I was really hoping to see my daughter, but if she's in Europe, I might as well . . ."

"Oh, Miss Charlene isn't in Europe, sir. She's at the yacht club this evening. She spends most evenings there."

Cody felt like shouting his pleasure. He wasn't going to see Emily, but he damn well would see his daughter without any interference. "Is my daughter married, Higgins?"

"No, sir, but I can tell you her mother wishes she were. She hangs around with all those worthless dandies, drinking and smoking too much, and staying out until all hours of the night. I don't know how she ever got through school leading such a life, but she did. She just graduated from Tomlinson's College."

Cody snorted. "Tomlinson's no more than a young lady's finishing school. All they care about is using the proper fork at a dinner party."

"I suppose you're right, sir," Higgins agreed with a smile, "but Miss Charlene is very intelligent, and her mother has taken her under her wing and is teaching her everything about the business."

"Just like her mother did," Cody snarled. "Nothing changes, does it, Higgins? The strong, dominating Van Payton women living in their own world without men. Listen to me." Cody laughed bitterly. "Old memories die hard, my friend. So many times I wondered what I could have done to change the way things worked out, but I guess that's water under the bridge."

"I suppose it is, sir, but I believe Miss Emily has often regretted what happened. She has definitely needed a man's firm hand with her daughter."

"Has she ever considered remarrying, Higgins?" Cody asked.

"No, sir, not that the men in San Francisco haven't tried. She's still a very beautiful woman, but most men find her intimidating." Higgins looked embarrassed, wondering if he'd said too much. "I mean, with all her money and power," he explained.

"I know what you mean," Cody said, remembering only too well how people responded to the Van Payton fortune. "It sounds like Emily was influenced by the old lady," he surmised bitterly. "Look, Higgins, I'd better be on my way. I'll come back tomorrow and talk to my daughter."

"If you'd like to see her tonight, I can call the

yacht club and tell them that you're a guest of Emily Van Payton. That way you could see Miss Charlene in her element."

"I don't think that's the best place for me to introduce myself," Cody said thoughtfully, "but maybe I could just observe her without her knowing it."

"I'll make the call, sir. Do you need the chauffeur to take you there? He's in the kitchen just waiting around for Miss Charlene to call for him."

"Thanks, Higgins, but I have a car."

Nothing much had changed at the yacht club. It had been redecorated, but it was still filled with a bunch of stuffed-shirt, pompous individuals, all trying to outdo each other in their financial games. Cody glanced around the room, then headed for the bar. He figured after nineteen years no one there was going to recognize him, but he still wanted to be as inconspicuous as possible. *Yeah, old man, inconspicuous in a Western tailored suit and cowboy boots. At least you had the sense enough to leave your hat in the car, even if you do feel naked without it.*

He ordered a beer, then swiveled his chair around to observe the people in the room. He focused on a lovely blonde surrounded by several young men—young *adolescents* would be more like it. None of them looked like they could fight their way out of a paper bag, much less satisfy a woman. He could tell the entire group had already had too much to drink. They were being loud and boisterous, disturbing the other diners in the room.

He was certain it was his daughter at the table, even though something deep within him hoped it wasn't. The resemblance to Emily was remarkable.

He watched as she drew a cigarette from a gold case and three of her admirers lit cigarette lighters at the same time. A moment later a waiter arrived at the table with their meals, only to get a scathing rebuke from the girl when he set the plate in front of her. Laughter followed the embarrassed waiter as he left with the plate of untouched food.

Cody sipped his beer glancing around the room, hoping there might be another young lady who resembled Emily. He sure as hell didn't like what he saw in this particular one. Emily might have been a snob, but she wasn't rude to people, and she didn't make a spectacle of herself in public.

"Well, hello there." A young redhead suddenly blocked his view of the table he was watching. "I don't believe I've seen you here before," she said, flashing him a brilliant smile. "I'm Lynn Barnes," she announced, offering him her hand.

"Cody Jones," he said, shaking her hand, "and you haven't seen me before because I haven't been here, at least not since you were born. I'm just visiting San Francisco."

"I thought as much. I was certain if you had been here before I would have noticed you among this priggish crowd. You are the best thing I've seen in here in a long time," she said, giving him a coquettish grin. "As a matter of fact, you're the best thing I've *ever* seen in here."

Cody forced a smile. He was used to women coming on to him, and usually enjoyed it. Strange how quickly your priorities changed when you knew you were going to die. "Why don't you let me buy you a drink, Lynn, and perhaps you can point out a few of the notables in attendance tonight."

"So, you're a people watcher," Lynn commented as she took the stool next to him. "I enjoy watching people, too. Sometimes I just sit at Ghirardelli Square and watch the people go by. I can tell you, it's a lot more fascinating than watching these snobs."

Cody laughed. "I thought you were one of them by the way you're dressed."

"My family has money now, but it's what San Franciscans call new money." She laughed. "My father made his fortune selling cars, and most of these people look down their noses at us."

"I can't imagine anyone in his right mind looking down his nose at you, Lynn. Why, you're the prettiest little filly here."

"Oh, I love how you talk, Cody," she giggled.

Suddenly the bartender appeared in front of them to take her order. "White wine?" Cody asked Lynn.

"Heavens no. I'd like a beer. Now let's see," she said, swiveling back around to look over the crowd. "The old fogies over there by the window are the Carlisles and the Dumonts, both old money. The next table is my mother and father, Sally and Lou Barnes, and my brother Al and his wife Muffy. She's one of the snobs, by the way."

"How about the table over there." Cody nodded toward the table where he was sure his daughter held court.

"The queen of the snobs," Lynn snorted. "That's Charlene Van Payton and her usual entourage."

Cody felt a lump in his throat as he watched one of the simpering idiots at the table fill his daughter's glass with champagne. "What's wrong with her?" he tentatively asked.

"Where do I start?" she joked, laughter in her eyes. "She's a spoiled brat, she thinks she's better than everyone else, and she uses people, as you can see from the way she keeps those young men jumping at her every command. Do you want me to go on?"

"Please."

"She always shows up here in a fur coat and all her jewels, smoking her cigarettes with a holder like they did in the thirties. I swear, I don't know who she thinks she's impressing," Lynn said, turning back to take a sip of her beer. "I think she's been watching too many old movies."

"Granted, she looks spoiled and pampered, but this tirade sounds a little like jealousy," Cody commented.

"Jealousy!" Lynn laughed. "I wouldn't want to be anything like that poor creature. She may have more money than anyone else in San Francisco, but she has little else. She spent the last four years of her life away at a private finishing school; she has no real friends, a mother who's too busy to pay her any attention; and God knows where her father is."

Cody swallowed with great difficulty. "What story does the family give about her father?"

Lynn took a sip of her beer. "I've never heard much about him, but you can believe if he was smart he took off running years ago. You should see the way Miss Van Payton treats the employees here at the club. They would rather deal with Attila the Hun than to get near her."

Cody wanted to defend his daughter, but how could he? She sounded like a carbon copy of her grandmother. His only consolation was that she looked bored, even though she was putting on a good show of being the life of the party. There had to be something he could do, short of having her hog-tied to get her away from this environment. That was all it would take, he was sure of it.

He lifted his glass to take a drink and his hand suddenly began to tremble, one of the symptoms of his illness. He quickly set the glass back down, but not before spilling beer all over his clothes.

"Are you all right?" Lynn asked, a puzzled expression on her face.

"Just sloppy," he said, glancing at his watch. "I better be on my way. It's been nice talking with you, Lynn."

"I'm sorry you have to leave so soon. I thought for a change I was going to enjoy an evening in this stuffy place."

"Why do you come here?" Cody asked as he tossed a twenty-dollar bill on the counter.

"It pleases my parents. They mean well," she shrugged, "but they're not satisfied just to have money. They think I should marry one of these snobs to give me respectability. What they don't realize is, I wouldn't take one of these wimps if they were wrapped up in ribbon and served on a silver platter. I see what marrying a snob has done to my brother. He's miserable trying to live up to his wife's standards."

"I know the feeling, Red," he said with a grin. "I tried it one time myself. Take some advice from a well-meaning stranger. Don't let it happen to you."

"I don't intend to, *stranger*," she grinned, "but thanks for the advice."

Cody sat in the parking lot waiting to get one more glimpse of his daughter. His hand still trembled and he'd had trouble remembering where he'd parked his car. The symptoms were getting worse and he sure as hell didn't want to be alone in San Francisco when his time came. Besides, it was going to take a lot more than introducing himself to his daughter to help her. It was going to take a miracle, but somehow he had to come up with some plan that would make her see there was more to life than partying, drinking, and using people.

TWO

SEPTEMBER

Emily Van Payton leaned her head against the plush leather chair, her eyes filled with tears. The telegram she had just received dropped to the floor. Cody was dead . . . Cody with the sweet smile and devastating charm. That must have been why he had been in San Francisco a few months ago. He had known he was dying and wanted to see his daughter, but why hadn't he? Higgins told her Cody had said he was going to come back the next morning, but he had never shown up, and she hadn't heard a word from him since.

"Cody, Cody," she whispered. "You were the only love in my life, and I threw it all away, and for what? To be a prisoner behind this desk with several thousand people depending on me to make the right decisions to keep things running smoothly. You were much wiser than I was, Cody, but I couldn't see it at the time."

She closed her eyes and remembered the first time

she had seen him sitting tall and straight in the saddle, his face tanned and his green eyes sparkling with mischief. The same green eyes that their daughter had. He had called her a tenderfoot and city slicker, but she had quickly learned to ride with his help—and to become a woman, with his expertise. She remembered that night they had sat before the campfire after everyone else had turned in. He was so experienced and so gentle with her . . .

Oh, God, what was she doing sitting here reminiscing. She had to tell Charlene.

She buzzed her secretary and asked that her daughter be sent to her office immediately. A few minutes later Charlene plopped down in the seat across from her, looking bored and impatient.

"What do you want, Mother? I was in an important meeting with Carlisle."

"This is more important. I just received this telegram," she said, passing the paper across the desk.

Charlene read the telegram and tossed it back on the desk. "So?"

Emily's eyes widened in surprise. "Charlene, the telegram says your father died several days ago."

Charlene took a cigarette from her gold case and lit it. "It says someone named Cody Jones died. I didn't know the man."

"The man was your father, Charlene. He deserves a little consideration and perhaps a moment of mourning from his daughter."

"A father cares for his children. This man cared nothing for me, and his death means nothing to me."

Emily stared at her dispassionate daughter, realizing it was her fault Charlene had never gotten the chance to know the man who was her father. She had let Agatha convince her that it would be traumatic for Charlene to be torn between the two of them, even if it was only during the summer months. Agatha was positive that it would be a terrifying experience for Charlene to spend a month in a primitive world she knew nothing about, and with people who were strangers to her.

Emily closed her eyes for a moment. "Charlene, there is something I should have told you before. Your father wasn't the only one at fault in our divorce."

Charlene looked at her watch and yawned. "Mother, this is all very interesting, but a little late, don't you think? If you want to mourn the man, go right ahead, but I have more important things to do."

"Charlene! This is your father I'm talking about. The least you can do is sit there and listen to me for a few minutes."

"What's the point now, Mother? Grandmama already told me he was a drifter and no-account rodeo rider who married you for your money."

"That's not true! Your father never took a cent of my money."

"That was because Grandmama didn't let him," Charlene said caustically. "Now if you're finished reminiscing, I have a meeting to get back to."

"How can you not show some emotion, Charlene?" Emily asked, bewildered. "The man was your father."

"The man is a stranger to me, Mother. I don't know what you expect. I'm twenty-one years old and this is the first time you've ever really spoken of him. The only information I had about him was from

Grandmama." She glanced at her watch again. "I really do need to get back to my meeting."

"Go," Emily sighed, sinking back in her chair as her daughter left her office.

Emily took a deep breath, trying to compose herself. It wasn't fair to lash out at Charlene for mistakes that were hers. How could her daughter possibly understand what she was feeling? The old memories and the guilt were suddenly so strong again. She had just wanted her daughter to understand that her father wasn't the villain in their marriage. He was a good man, and she'd often regretted her decision. She should have been stronger and stood up to her mother, but she hadn't. She and Charlene would both have been better off if they'd forgotten the Van Payton fortune and gone to the mountains with Cody.

"Oh, Cody, what have I done?" she whispered out loud. "I've ruined three lives with my selfishness and greed. The only time in my life I was happy was when I was with you. And now I watch our daughter making the same mistakes I made, letting money and power take precedence over everything else. I didn't mean for it to turn out this way. I always thought someday, together as friends, you and I would enjoy our daughter, but time got away from me, Cody—time, precious time. Why is it we waste so much of it doing things we really don't want to do?"

Emily smiled. "You didn't, though, did you, Cody? You went back to Wyoming, to the life you loved, while I stayed here under my mother's thumb, being controlled and smothered, hating every day, and look at me. I've done the same thing to Charlene, and I don't know what to do about it. She really isn't so bad, Cody. She has too much of my mother in her, but she has her good points, too. Unfortunately, in this environment she's had little opportunity to show it. Oh, God, Cody, what can I do before it's too late?''

A knock at the door interrupted her thoughts. She wiped the tears from her eyes and called for her secretary to enter.

Mary stared at her, a concerned look on her usually stern face. ''Miss Van Payton, are you all right?''

''Yes, thank you, Mary.''

''A special delivery envelope just arrived, Miss Van Payton. It's from a lawyer in Jackson, Wyoming.''

Emily felt a lump in her throat. ''Thank you, Mary. Please don't let anyone disturb me until I tell you.''

''What about your two o'clock appointment with Mr. Tanner?''

''Postpone it until tomorrow. Tell him I've had a family emergency.''

When she was alone Emily slowly opened the envelope. There was a brief letter from the lawyer, a hand-written letter from Cody, and some legal documents. Emily glanced at the lawyer's letter first, then picked up Cody's letter, touching it to her lips before reading.

Dear Emily,

I tried to see you a few months ago, but you were in Europe. I had hoped to have the opportunity to meet my daughter, but circumstances prevented it. I did have an opportunity to observe her with her friends, and I'm sorry to say, what I saw didn't particularly please me. She reminded me very much of your mother, with her superior attitude and rudeness to people she felt were beneath her. I had hoped you would raise her differently, Emily, but perhaps you're too close to the situation to see the flaws.

I left San Francisco determined to do something to help my daughter see that there is another way of life, a life where people aren't judged by how much money they have or what kind of car they drive. My plan is going to need your help, Emily. I hope what we once had together will persuade you to go along with my last wishes.

I am leaving Charlene half of my ranch. The other half will go to my longtime friend and partner, Zach Leighton, a hard-working, well-educated young man who has been like a son to me. I have stipulated in my will that before she can sell her half, which I'm sure will be her first reaction, she has to spend at least two weeks there. If she is still determined to sell out at that time, she has to sell to Zach. I realize that legally I can't force her to go to Wyoming, but that's where you come into my plan. I'm depending on you to convince her it is the only decent thing to do.

By now you may be cussing me for being a nervy bastard, but I hope not. What I'm asking is not so unreasonable. If you think about it, I could have forced you to let me share custody of our daughter when she was young, but I didn't. Do this for me now, Emily, in memory of what we once shared. Give our daughter a chance to have what we so briefly had. I remember a beautiful, sophisticated young lady who thought a horseback ride in the moonlight was pretty special. I've been remembering a lot of things these past few months about our time together. We could have had a good life together, Emily, if we hadn't let so many outsiders interfere. Let's try to give our daughter a chance to see my way of life. Maybe she'll find it to her liking. I've never been one to believe in miracles, but it can't hurt to hope for this one.

Take care of yourself, my beautiful Emily, and be happy. Life is too short not to enjoy it.

Emily laughed through her tears. "Ah, Cody, you were a step ahead of me. Yes, I will see that Charlene has no choice but to abide by your wishes."

After meeting with her lawyer, Jeremy Grenville, and explaining to him what she wanted, they came up with a plan. A few days later she was ready to tell Charlene about her father's will and his wishes. Knowing her daughter as she did, she knew it was still going to be an uphill battle—and she was so right.

"The last thing I need is a cow farm in some godforsaken part of the country!" Charlene exclaimed. "Tell his partner that he can have the whole thing. I want nothing to do with it."

"Now, Charlene, don't make a hasty decision you'll regret. I want you to hear what Jeremy has discovered about Hawk's Cry Ranch."

"I don't care if he found out it's the Taj Mahal. I don't want anything to do with it."

"And you don't have to accept your father's gift if you don't wish to," the lawyer commented, "but to avoid a long drawn-out legal battle, it would be best if you did as the will stipulates. After two weeks you can sell your share to this partner, if that is still your wish. Personally, after the research I've done, I think you might want to hold on to the property."

"Why on earth would I want to do that?"

"My research shows the ranch is a bit rustic, but it has one of the most beautiful settings in Wyoming."

"That's very nice," she said, with little enthusiasm. "I understand Alaska is beautiful, too, but I have no desire to go there."

"You wanted to do something important for the company, Charlene," her mother pointed out. "I'll give you this opportunity to check the place out for its potential as a Van Payton resort. You've been dabbling in our resort properties and should know that ranches in isolated areas are very popular with the affluent set. Jeremy tells me everything in that part of the country is rustic, usually a dude ranch-type facility. We could completely rebuild the place, add an indoor pool, Jacuzzi, steam and sauna rooms, have aerobic programs and gourmet meals. It could become a very exclusive spa that the rich and famous would flock to."

Forgive me, Cody, Emily thought silently, *but it's the only way I know to get her there. I promise, no matter what happens, I won't change your ranch.*

Charlene was still silent, thinking about what her mother and Jeremy had said. She had been wanting a chance to prove to her mother that she could handle the business, and this would also be a way to show her friends that she not only had money, but that she was as intelligent as her mother and grandmother and could run Van Payton Enterprises when her time came. Perhaps this was the opportunity she needed. What an accomplishment it would be to develop this ranch into an exclusive spa/resort where the rich could go to be pampered while they enjoyed the scenery.

"What do you think, darling? Can you handle this?" Emily asked, hoping her daughter would take the challenge.

"Of course I can handle it, but I can't go until next week. I promised Lawrence I would attend the Pavarotti concert with him, and I don't want to miss it. Besides, I'll need a few new outfits. Perhaps some new designer jeans and a few cashmere sweaters. I've been wanting a new pink one. That fool Joshua ruined the one I have," she said in disgust.

"That should be fine," Emily said with relief, "but I would suggest you pack warm clothes."

"Mother, this is still September!" Charlene exclaimed.

"I know, dear, but winter comes early to that part of the country."

"Fine. I'll be able to put my new fur coat to use. I don't suppose there will be any social affairs going on at the ranch, but I'll take a couple of cocktail dresses just in case."

Emily smiled to herself. "Yes, you do that, dear."

THREE

The private jet of Van Payton Enterprises set down on the runway of the Jackson Hole airport and deposited its one passenger before quickly taking off.

Charlene made her way to a counter in the terminal and asked where she could get a limousine. The woman behind the counter looked up in surprise.

"I'm sorry, ma'am," she said after a moment. "There isn't a limo service here. Most of the ranches send their own vehicles in to pick up guests during peak season. Tell me where you're staying and I'll be glad to see if I can get someone to come for you."

Charlene sighed in exasperation and began searching through her briefcase. "It's some ridiculous name like Bird Call Ranch or some such thing. Here it is. Hawk's Cry Ranch."

"Oh, I'm sorry, ma'am, but they've closed up for the season. They are up pretty high in the mountains and already have had a couple of snows."

"I have to get there somehow," Charlene said impatiently. "What am I supposed to do?"

"I don't know, ma'am. We're pretty much at the mercy of the weather here," she tried to explain.

"This is ridiculous! What kind of way is this to run an airport? I want to talk to someone in authority here."

"That would be Evan Jamerson, but he's up in the mountains skiing."

"Oh, for God's sake," Charlene fumed in exasperation.

"There is one possibility," the girl mused. "You might be able to rent a four-wheel-drive vehicle, but I doubt it. We're expecting our first big snow of the season and Chuck is very protective of his vehicles when it comes to outsiders using them, particularly when you're talking about going as far up into the mountains as you are."

"Point out this *Chuck* and I'll deal with him," Charlene said haughtily. "Someone around this place has to have some business sense."

"He's at the last counter on the left, ma'am. If you like, you can leave your luggage here until you have everything settled. Just tell Chuck that Dallas is keeping your luggage for you. He knows who I am."

Charlene's stiletto heels clicked loudly as she made her way to the counter that the girl had pointed out. "What are you looking at?" she asked irritably as she passed a cowboy who stared at her with a look of disbelief on his face. "Haven't you ever seen a lady before?"

"No, ma'am, 'spose I haven't," he said, tipping

his hat to her. "Least ways, not one dressed like you."

Charlene tried to ignore the crowd of similarly dressed men who seemed to gather around as she stepped up to the counter. The only person there had his feet propped up on a chair and was reading a girlie magazine. "I assume you're Chuck," she said.

"Yes, ma'am," he answered, getting to his feet. He leaned over the counter looking her up and down from her high heels to her sophisticated coiffed blond head. He gave an appreciative whistle. "I thought your type usually went to Vail or St. Moritz to ski."

"I am not here to ski," she retorted in annoyance. "I need a car to get me to Hawk's Cry Ranch. Preferably one with a driver. I'm willing to pay handsomely."

"I'm sorry, ma'am, but the latest weather report says a big snow is only a few hours away. I don't know anyone who wants to get stuck up in the mountains for the duration. I'm not even sure I want one of my vehicles to go up there."

"I'll pay you double what you usually get," Charlene said, pulling out her gold American Express card.

"I don't know, ma'am. Fact is, Hawk's Cry is already closed for the season."

"I'm well aware of that fact. It doesn't matter, I have to get there. I'll pay you triple what you usually get."

"You drive a hard bargain, little lady," he said, scratching his head. "I suppose I can let you have old Bessie."

"Old Bessie?" she repeated. "My good man, I didn't ask for a horse. I asked for a car."

"Old Bessie is a jeep, ma'am," he explained. "She's old, but she'll get you there."

"Fine. I'll need directions, and someone to put my luggage in old . . . the car?" she corrected, determined not to sink to the level of this annoying cowboy. "Do you think you can handle that?" she asked patronizingly.

"No problem, little lady. Why don't you get yourself a cup of coffee over there in the snack bar and I'll have old Bessie gassed up and brought around front."

"My luggage is with someone named Dallas a few counters from here."

"I'll take care of it," he assured her. "Just don't you worry about a thing."

Zach Leighton was nailing the final board over a window of one of the cabins to protect it from the snowstorm that was predicted, when he heard gears grinding as a vehicle came up the mountain. "Now what fool would be coming up here with the threat of a major snowstorm?" he mumbled as he hammered the last nail in. The sky was already dark with a purple tinge, and there was a silence that seemed to echo every little sound, a sure sign that the snow would be starting soon. He grimaced as the gears made a terrible sound. What the hell was that guy doing to his car?

As Zach rounded the corner of the lodge he stopped dead in his tracks. Emerging from a jeep that looked like it was an antique from World War I was a beautiful young lady dressed in a full-length mink coat, her blond hair styled in elegant curls and piled on top of her head. She teetered on spike high heels as she perilously made her way across the gravel driveway toward the door of the lodge. This was all he needed, he thought irritably. Some fancy woman who had lost her way in these mountains, who couldn't even drive her vehicle without stripping the gears.

"Can I help you with something, lady?" he asked, unable to keep the annoyance from his voice.

"Yes," she answered, looking him over from his cowboy boots to his cowboy hat. "You can get my bags out of that monster they call a car and take them to the owner's suite."

Zach closed his eyes and shook his head. This could be none other than Cody's socialite daughter. After reading Cody's will he'd known he'd have to deal with her sooner or later, but he certainly hadn't expected it to be until spring—and here she was on the brink of a major snowstorm.

Zach took his hat off and ran his hand through his dark hair before placing it back on his head. "Lady, if you're smart you'll get back in that jeep and get the hell out of here before it starts snowing."

Charlene's eyes widened. "How dare you. Do you know who you're talking to?" she asked indignantly.

"Yeah," he drawled, "I know who I'm talking to, but it doesn't make a damned bit of difference. If you don't want to be stranded on this mountain, I suggest you leave now."

Charlene stared at the dark-haired man with the angry blue eyes. Who did this ranch hand think he was? she wondered, her anger making her face turn pink. *Stay in control,* her grandmama had always told her. She forced a patient, condescending smile before speaking. "Either you *don't* know who you're talking to, or you don't value your job, young man." The cowboy had the audacity to laugh at her, making her even angrier.

"Lady, I'm not your *young man,*" he growled angrily. "And from descriptions I've heard you can be none other than the poor little rich girl who demands and commands her way through life, Ms. Charlene Van Payton, the long-lost daughter who finally shows up after her father is dead."

Charlene's face was now red with anger. "I don't know who you are, but you are fired as of this moment."

Zach laughed. "You're not in San Francisco, *Lady* Van Payton. I happen to be Zach Leighton, your partner, and I don't take orders from you or anyone else."

Charlene looked him over with contempt. "Well, we'll see if we can remedy that immediately," she said, turning back toward the lodge. "I'll write you a check for this worthless place and then you can leave."

"You can write all the damned checks you want, but I'm not going anywhere."

Charlene turned around and stared at him. "You have no idea what I'm willing to offer you for this godforsaken place. Now go on," she said, waving her hand to dismiss him. "Get my bags and take them to the owner's suite, then we'll talk business. I think you'll be pleasantly surprised when you hear my offer," she said smugly as she entered the lodge.

Zach stared after her. "My God, Cody's description of you didn't even come close," he swore angrily as he headed for the jeep. He'd known she was an arrogant, irritating shrew before she'd even opened her mouth. "Dammit, lady, if you weren't Cody's daughter! Owner's suite!" he mumbled to himself.

Zach dragged the expensive bags out of the jeep, wondering what he had ever done to Cody to deserve this. What in the world had the man been thinking about when he made them partners in the ranch? When Cody returned from San Francisco he had told him how disappointed he had been with his daughter, that she was spoiled and pampered beyond belief, so why would he force her to come to this secluded place? It was already obvious to him that she would never fit in. He had even offered to buy Cody out so the daughter could have her inheritance, but Cody had refused. Now he was beginning to wonder what his old friend had been up to. No good, that was for damned sure, he thought as he headed toward the lodge, carrying her fancy suitcases. "God, it looks like she packed to stay a while," he growled.

FOUR

Charlene was glancing around the lodge thinking rustic was an understatement. The room had a high cathedral ceiling with log beams supporting the roof. Rough-hewn logs made up the walls of the room, instead of the usual painted plaster or wallpaper. A large natural gray stone fireplace with a raised hearth took up almost an entire wall, and to each side of it were filled bookcases. The mantel was a thick piece of timber and a giant rack of some kind of animal's antlers hung above it. The only thing in the room she could see worth saving were the beautiful paintings of wildlife that decorated the walls.

I'll have to tear this whole place down and start over, she thought to herself. Suddenly her Gucci bags were dropped in a pile at her feet, startling her.

Her expensive perfume already permeated the room and made Zach's senses reel, which infuriated him even more.

"I'm going to warn you again that a snowstorm

is expected any time now," he said sharply, "and if you don't get off this mountain you could be here for weeks, maybe even months."

If he hadn't treated her with such disdain, she would have taken his advice and headed back to the airport, but she wasn't about to let this arrogant, rude, uneducated cowboy send her packing. "If you think you're frightening me, Mr. Leighton, you're not. In this day and age of four-wheel-drive vehicles, no one would get snowed in for months. Besides, I'm not going anywhere until you tell me what you want for your share of the ranch."

"There's no way in hell I'm going to sell out to you and let you turn your father's pride and joy into a slick jet-set resort."

She offered him an exorbitant amount of money, sure he wouldn't refuse. "Well, what do you have to say, Mr. Leighton?" she asked smugly.

"Keep your money, lady. I'm not selling."

Charlene's green eyes widened in astonishment. She had never met anyone who couldn't be bought if the price was right. It was something she had learned very early from her grandmother. "You aren't very bright, are you, Mr. Leighton?"

"No, ma'am, I 'spose not," he drawled in his best cowboy slang routine. If she wanted to think she was dealing with an idiot, let her. He was nobody's fool and she'd soon learn that.

"Listen, Mr. Leighton, money is no object to me," she said as she placed a cigarette in her gold holder and waited for him to light it. When he made no move to do so, she sighed in disgust and lit it herself. "I'll give you whatever you want for this place. Just name your price. Everyone has a price."

"I'd prefer it if you didn't . . ." He was about to tell her he didn't want her smoking when he glanced out the window. "Damnit, I warned you!" he shouted. "It's already started snowing. You've got about five minutes to get your . . . to get off this mountain, lady, or you're here for the duration, and I don't think you want that any more than I do."

"Nonsense," she laughed naively. "It's a little snow, and I am driving a four-wheel-drive vehicle. Now stop worrying about me, Mr. Leighton. I can take care of myself."

"I wasn't worrying about you, Lady Van Payton. I was concerned for my own privacy and sanity. I look forward to my time alone."

"And I'm sure the world appreciates that, Mr. Leighton, so if you want to get rid of me, name your price."

"I'm not selling," Zach said again as he threw several logs on the fire.

"You are the most hard-headed, irritating man I've ever met," Charlene shouted, losing her cool, which she had been taught never to do. She took a deep breath to compose herself. "Perhaps it would be best if you slept on my last offer, Mr. Leighton. I'm really very tired myself, so if you'll just show me to my suite we'll continue this discussion in the morning when we're both refreshed. I believe I'll take my dinner in my room. Just knock on the door when it's ready."

Zach had to laugh at the audacity of the woman. "Lady, what you see is what you get. This one room in the lodge is the only place that hasn't been closed up and winterized, and for your information, Hawk's

Cry Ranch doesn't offer room service even during the season.''

''You can't be serious?'' When he didn't answer she realized he was. ''Well, that's something we're certainly going to change very quickly. Any decent resort would offer room service.''

''I keep telling you, lady, this isn't a resort. And I hope you brought a sleeping bag with you,'' he said as he plopped down into an overstuffed chair in front of the roaring fire and picked up a book. ''It gets mighty cold on the floor.''

''Are you telling me that this one room is the only place where I can sleep . . . where we both will sleep?''

''If you don't want to freeze to death, it is.''

''What kind of a place is this?'' she asked, staring at him in disbelief.

''It's a ranch, ma'am,'' he said with that sarcastic drawl that irritated her to the quick. ''It's a place where the common folk come to enjoy the peace and quiet. I don't rightly think anyone like you has ever been here before, and I might add, you're about as welcome as a polecat at a picnic.''

''This is absurd. I insist you prepare one of the cottages I passed on the way up the mountain.''

''They're not cottages, ma'am. They're cabins, and they've been boarded up and winterized,'' he retorted, trying to keep his impatience in check. ''If you leave right now you can probably still make your way back down the mountain and find yourself a nice cozy room, but if you wait any longer . . .''

''I am not leaving until we settle our business,'' she said with trepidation as she glanced out the window at the fury of the snow coming down.

"As far as I'm concerned, there is no business to settle, ma'am. You made your offer, I refused it. Shucks, ma'am, what more could we have to talk about, unless you want to know about your father, or hadn't that even crossed your mind?"

Charlene's face turned red. "Cody Jones may have impregnated my mother, but he certainly wasn't a father to me."

"Did you ever wonder why?"

"I will not discuss this with you," she said as she jerked one of her suitcases open.

So, there is vulnerability there, he thought silently. *Maybe Cody had sensed that.* "Here," he said, tossing her a sleeping bag. "If you insist on staying the night, you can sleep on the couch. I don't intend to give up my bed."

"That's fine, but I would enjoy something to eat," she said haughtily.

"I made some stew earlier," he said, about to tell her where she could find it, but before he did, she collapsed into one of the big overstuffed chairs in front of the fireplace.

"I'm starved and exhausted. I have never had such a trying experience in all my life. No one in this godforsaken place wants to help you. I had to practically buy that decrepit piece of machinery just to get up here, because every fool at the airport insisted I couldn't make it."

Zach shook his head. "Did you ever stop to think perhaps they knew what they were talking about? People in this area don't have to listen to a weatherman. They read the sky and the clouds. Any fool would have known the snow was coming."

"I've seen snow before," she shrugged her shoulders. "What's the problem?"

Zach gritted his teeth as he headed for the kitchen. He'd get her something to eat this time, but then she was out of here in the morning, whether she was Cody's daughter or not.

A few minutes later he reappeared and handed her a tray with a bowl of stew and a large piece of bread. "It's plain and simple," he said, "but it's filling."

She dug into the stew with a ravenous appetite. "This is really very good. I've never had anything like it."

"You're kidding," he said. "No, I guess you're not. I don't imagine the Van Payton menu has Irish stew on it."

"Aren't you going to eat?" she asked, feeling uneasy as he watched her.

"Already did."

"I'd really like another bowl, if you don't mind, and another piece of that delicious bread. When I take this place over, I'll have to be sure to get the name of the bakery you use," she said as he headed back toward the kitchen. "This bread is wonderful."

Zach shook his head in disgust as he left the room. Moments later he set the bowl of stew and bread in front of her "It didn't come from a bakery, Lady Van Payton. I baked it myself."

Charlene laughed, thinking he was kidding.

"What's so funny?" he asked defensively.

"You're not serious about baking the bread."

"I'm very serious. When you live alone in the wilderness six months or more out of the year, you learn to do stuff like that, or do without."

"You live alone six months at a time?" she asked, her green eyes wide with disbelief.

"Someone has to stay here and take care of the place," he said as he poured them coffee. "I did it last year, and I plan to do it this year, if I can get rid of you."

"Don't worry, Mr. Leighton, I'll be out of your hair as soon as we settle our business. Just think about it. Accept my offer and you'll never have to stay here alone again. You can take your money and buy a place in Arizona, or California, someplace where you don't get snowed in for months at a time. Who knows, maybe if you were off this mountain you could meet a nice young lady who could teach you some manners."

"Shucks, ma'am, you mean you think I might be able to find me a purty little heifer in the big city. I have to admit, I've thought about ordering me a mail-order bride," he lied, trying to keep a straight face. "One as pretty as a bouquet of daisies."

"Oh, my word, Mr. Leighton," she said in disgust, "if that's the way you talk to women, you'll never find one who would be interested in you."

Zach had to grin as he added another log to the fire. "Then maybe I better stay right where I am, ma'am. The wildlife around here don't seem to mind the way I talk."

Charlene shook her head, unable to believe anyone would live like this. "Didn't Mr. Jones stay here during the winter?" she asked as she popped the last of the bread into her mouth.

"Your father," he emphasized the words, "always stayed here until last year. He wasn't feeling well and

decided to spend the off-season in Arizona, so I stayed here, and thoroughly enjoyed the peace and quiet."

"What in the world do you do?"

"Read, listen to music, take walks, paint."

"I'd go insane," she exclaimed.

"That's why I keep warning you to leave, Ms. Van Payton. You better hope it stops snowing by morning so you can get off this mountain."

"Don't worry, Mr. Leighton, I'll leave as soon as we conclude our business," she assured him as she set the tray on the table next to her. "Now if you will be so kind as to point me toward the powder room, I think I will prepare for bed."

"You'll have to tell me what a powder room is," he said, pretending ignorance. "I don't believe we have one."

"Oh, God," she sighed, looking at the ceiling. "The bathroom, Mr. Leighton. Where is the bathroom? You know, the room where you wash your face and brush your teeth. I assume you do those things, even living like a hermit in this godforsaken place."

"Well, I'll tell you, ma'am, I bathe and clean my teeth in the stream that runs behind the lodge. It's as invigorating as a good roll in the . . . well, it's invigorating, if you get my drift. You'll have to try it in the mornin'."

"Oh, no!" she exclaimed, a horrified look on her face. "Outside . . . You wash and . . . and . . . outside?"

"Yes, ma'am," he grinned, "but if you prefer, there is a bathroom right down the hallway."

"Thank God for small favors," she sighed, with relief.

"And by the way, you can wash your dishes in

the kitchen right through that door." He pointed behind her.

"Wash my dishes?" she repeated. "But I . . . I mean . . . Of course," she said, picking up the tray.

Zach nearly laughed aloud. It was obvious Lady Van Payton had never washed a dish in her life, but she wasn't going to admit it. He was surprised when he heard the water run and dishes rattle as they were being washed. Maybe if she thought she'd have to wash her own dishes she'd hightail it off his mountain. "Powder room," he mumbled as he stared out the window at the snow. Wait until she discovered how cold it was in the *powder room.* He usually turned a heater on, but why spoil her, he thought, smiling to himself. He sure hoped she didn't need to sit on the toilet seat. He had to suppress his laughter when he thought about what a shock it would be for the princess from San Francisco.

"Excuse me, but where will I find towels?" Charlene asked as she headed toward the bathroom.

"There's a closet just outside the bathroom door, ma'am. You'll find some in there."

Zach picked up a magazine and flipped through it, waiting for her to return, so he could do battle with her again when she complained about the bath facilities, but the words froze on his lips as he stared at the tall, statuesque beauty dressed in a clinging black nightgown. She had brushed her blond hair out and it now seemed to shimmer like gold as the firelight played off it. "Very appropriate attire, Lady Van Payton," he mumbled, turning back toward the fireplace. "Just what the well-dressed woman wears to be snowed in on a mountaintop for the winter. I sure hope you have more appropriate clothes in those fancy suitcases.''

The haughty angle to her head told him she hadn't before she answered.

"I thought I was coming to a decent resort, Mr. Leighton. I'm afraid I'm not very well prepared for mountain living. I brought several cocktail dresses, several more nightgowns, a few sweaters and skirts, and one pair of jeans. Believe me, if I'd have known how cold this place would be, I'd have packed something different,'' she retorted. "That bathroom is like a freezer.'' She straightened out the sleeping bag, studying each end. "This whole place is like something out of the past.''

"It's a tough life, lady,'' Zach muttered as he prepared to get into his bed. "I'm sure those cocktail dresses will come in real handy.'' Out of the corner of his eye he watched her trying to figure out how to get into her sleeping bag.

"Whoever invented this thing must have been a contortionist,'' she said in frustration.

"Unzip it and slide in,'' he instructed, impatience obvious in his voice. "Then you can zip it up from the inside.'' *Beauty and no brains,* he thought to himself.

"This thing is supposed to keep me warm?''

"I can't say with what you have on, ma'am,'' he answered in disgust. "Only a greenhorn would come to Jackson Hole, Wyoming, in late September without warm clothes.''

"As I said, if I'd had any idea this place was something from the Dark Ages, I would have brought appropriate clothes. No. I retract that statement. If I had known what this place was like, I wouldn't have let myself be talked into this fiasco.''

"Now, why doesn't it surprise me that you didn't come out of any sentimental obligation to your father?" he said sarcastically.

"If my father had felt anything for me, he would have made it a point to seek me out," she retorted.

"I know for a fact he tried often," Zach said as he turned off his light.

"That's your story, Mr. Leighton," she answered, her teeth chattering. "My God, it's cold in here. Can't you set the thermostat a little higher?"

Zach laughed. "Sorry, Lady Van Payton. The only heat we have is the fireplace and the woodstove in the kitchen."

"I can't believe anyone lives like this," she grumbled. "If I were in San Francisco right now, I'd be preparing to attend the Octoberfest that's going to be held at the yacht club."

"We can't all be rich and pampered," he commented. "And thank God for that."

"Anyone in their right mind would prefer that life to this," she snapped.

Zach heard her unzip her bag. "What are you doing?"

"I'm going to get my fur coat," she informed him. "Maybe that will help keep me warm."

"Yeah, you may as well put it to good use, since all those cute little animals gave their lives so you could parade around in their fur."

"Oh, God, don't tell me you're one of those," she moaned as she struggled to get back into her sleeping bag.

"You're damned right I am. I believe in live and let live. If you ever saw one of those creatures I'd bet you'd think twice before buying a fur coat."

"Well, since I've never seen one, and don't plan to, I'll just enjoy what I have."

"Yeah, like they say, ignorance is bliss."

"I know your type, Mr. Leighton," she said sarcastically. "You can't afford to buy fur so you pretend to be an animal rights activist when it suits you. I noticed there was meat in the stew, so you're not against killing animals for food."

"No, I'm not, but I'm against killing them needlessly so some selfish woman can wear their fur."

"That's what I thought. You're a hypocrite," she accused him, suddenly throwing the sleeping bag aside. "I can't deal with this thing," she whined. "I don't fit into it with my coat on, and I'm freezing."

"Oh, for God's sake," he exclaimed, getting out of his bed. "I'm tired of listening to you. You take the bed tonight and I'll sleep on the couch in the sleeping bag."

Instead of thanking him, she said, "Well, I think that's only fair since I am a guest."

Zach clenched his fist and closed his eyes, praying for patience. "I suggest you go to sleep, before I'm forced to do something I'll end up in the electric chair for," he warned.

"What is that supposed to mean?" she asked, snuggling down under the warm comforter.

"Don't ask. Just go to sleep. You have a long trip ahead of you in the morning."

Zach pulled the sleeping bag up over his head, trying not to think of the way she looked in that slinky black nightgown. He sure hoped she'd be able to get off the mountain in the morning because he didn't know how he was going to deal with this selfish, thoughtless scatterbrain with the face and body of an angel and the personality of the devil himself.

FIVE

Charlene woke up to find Zach putting wood on the fire. He didn't have a shirt on and his hair was still wet, apparently from his dip in the stream he'd mentioned. She wasn't used to seeing men walking around half naked, and she could feel the heat rise to her face. His jeans clung to his well-muscled legs and the curve of his hips. She felt a strange sensation in the pit of her stomach and told herself it had to be hunger pains. "Did it stop snowing?" she asked, stretching her arms out from under the covers as she forced her thoughts away from his broad shoulders and narrow waistline.

"Look for yourself," he answered shortly, as he slipped a sweater over his head.

Charlene sat up and slipped into her fur coat before placing her bare feet on the cold floor. "Oh, my God!" she exclaimed as she stared out the window at the snow already up to the bottom of the window. "I can't believe this."

"I tried to warn you," Zach said irritably, "but you wouldn't listen. You come up here from San Francisco without a clue as to what you were facing, then act surprised when it snows. You oughta get out in the world more often, Lady Van Payton."

"Just calm down, Mr. Leighton. We'll discuss business over breakfast and then I'll leave."

Zach laughed bitterly. "Sure you will. Have you bothered to take a good look at your jeep?"

Charlene glanced out the window again. "It's covered with snow," she said, as if that weren't a problem. "Surely a big strong man like yourself can shovel me out. If not, I'll call the American Automobile Association to come and get me."

"Oh, God!" Zach exclaimed, throwing his hands up in exasperation. "I'm going to check things out," he announced, grabbing his coat off the peg on the wall. "You'll find everything you need in the kitchen to make flapjacks. I'll take a big stack and at least three sausage cakes, and I like my coffee strong."

Charlene's eyes widened, then she laughed. "Now just a moment. I've been in a kitchen one time in my life and that was to get an ice pack for a hangover. I have no idea how to cook flapjacks, or even know what they are."

"Damn," he hissed, throwing his coat down. "Get dressed. Then I'll show you how to fix breakfast this morning, but you better take a crash course with a cookbook, lady, because if you stay here you're going to pull your weight."

"I have no intention of staying here, Mr. Leighton," she said as she slipped her fur coat off and picked through her suitcase for something to wear. "I keep telling you that all you have to do is agree to sell me your half of this ranch and I'll be on my way, leaving you to your peace and solitude."

"You already have my answer on selling out to you," he said, forcing his eyes from her slender body encased in black satin. He sighed in disgust at himself. How was it possible a bit of satin and lace could make a sensible man start having ridiculous thoughts even when he couldn't stand the woman? So she was beautiful, with a flawless face and figure. The woman was a cold, selfish bitch and he'd better remember that. God, maybe he had been on this mountain too long, he thought silently. "Your father loved this place and I won't see it ruined."

"I have no intention of ruining it. I plan to make it one of the most elaborate, state-of-the-art spas and resorts in this part of the country," she explained. "I'll add an indoor swimming pool and spa that resembles a Roman bath, and I'll build new cottages, all white and pink, each overlooking a beautiful garden, and I'll add tennis courts, and putting greens, and . . ."

"It sounds just *glorious,*" he said, mocking her. "Just what a person comes to the mountains of Wyoming for. I'll be in the kitchen. Join me when you're dressed," he ordered.

As he put a pot of coffee on he wondered if the girl looked like her mother. That would certainly explain why Cody had been swept off his feet. It was a damned shame the personality didn't fit the face and figure.

"All right, Mr. Leighton," she said as she entered the kitchen. "What do you want me to do?"

Zach looked up from the coffeepot. She was dressed in tight-fitting designer jeans and a soft pink sweater that outlined her small but perfect breasts. "What, no cocktail dress?" he said irritably.

She glanced around. The kitchen was large, yet it had a cozy feeling to it. A large wood stove occupied a corner and modern appliances and a round oak table filled the rest of the room.

"You have an attitude problem, Mr. Leighton."

"Yeah, I suppose I do," he agreed as he placed an egg in her hand. "Break the egg into that bowl and mix it while I get the flour and buttermilk."

"Buttermilk? Yuk," Charlene exclaimed as she stared at the egg in her hand.

"It makes the best flapjacks," he explained as he gathered the rest of the ingredients. "There are several cookbooks on the shelf. I suggest you spend your extra time studying them. I don't mind a little experimentation if you want to try out some of the dishes."

"I'll be leaving soon, Mr. Leighton, so you'll have to do your own cooking," she said as she dropped the egg in the bowl and began to mix it, shell and all.

Zach stared at her, then the bowl, in disbelief. "I can't believe anyone could be so . . . so dense."

"How dare you. I'll have you know I can run a business better than any man."

"Yeah, well, you'd have a hard time convincing me of that, lady, because you don't know a damned thing about taking care of yourself. If I weren't on this mountain you would have frozen, or starved to death, by now. Anybody who can't even crack an egg . . ." he mumbled as he dumped the egg and shell out of the bowl.

"Mr. Leighton, I have two cooks, three maids, a

butler, and a chauffeur. Why in the world would I want to learn to be domestic?''

''Everyone should be able to take care of themselves, Lady Van Payton. Look at the situation you find yourself in right now. I sure as hell am not going to play nursemaid to you while you're here. You're going to pull your own weight, just like I do, and you're going to begin right now by learning to fix a decent breakfast.''

Charlene continued to glare at him, but said nothing. ''First we need to get our sausage cakes on,'' he said, going to the freezer. ''They are already in patties, so all you have to do is place them in that black skillet on a low flame.'' He tossed the package to her. ''I'll pour us a cup of coffee, then we'll work together to get the flapjacks mixed.''

''I'll humor you this time, Mr. Leighton, but I'm out of here after breakfast.''

''I can't think of anything that would make me happier, Lady Van Payton,'' he said, thinking the woman had as much warmth as an icicle, and he couldn't imagine having to spend the winter with her.

Charlene glared at him. He was the rudest, most obnoxious, irritating man she'd ever met. ''I would appreciate it if you would stop calling me Lady Van Payton.''

''Would you prefer Princess Van Payton?''

''I would prefer Ms. Van Payton,'' she said between gritted teeth.

''I'll try to remember that. Now, this is the way you break an egg,'' he explained as he cracked the shell on the side of the bowl and let the contents drop into it. ''Now we mix it and set it aside, then in another bowl mix together flour, baking soda, baking powder, sugar, and salt. Now to the egg mixture we add buttermilk and oil.''

''This sounds terribly complicated,'' Charlene complained. ''I'm sure if flapjacks were worth all this trouble, I would have had them before now.''

Zach ignored her complaints. ''We could use a mix, but I found doing it from scratch is much better. Now we mix the egg mixture into the flour mixture and we're ready to start cooking them.''

''Wonderful,'' she mumbled sarcastically.

''This is a griddle,'' he explained, holding up the flat pan as if talking to a child. ''We lightly grease it, let it get hot, and then put about a fourth of a cup of batter on it in dollops, like this. When the tops start bubbling we turn them over. Are you getting all of this?'' he asked, wondering why she was suddenly so quiet.

''Listen, Mr. Leighton, I'm just not cut out to be a cook, so I'll tell you what I'll do. I'll double the offer I made you and I can be on my way and you can cook breakfast to your heart's content.''

Zach's blue eyes flashed angrily. ''Lady, you could offer me every cent Van Payton Enterprises has and I still wouldn't sell to you. Cody Jones was like a father to me, and I intend to respect his wishes.''

''I'm glad he was a father to someone,'' Charlene spat.

''He was also my friend,'' he said, glaring at her. ''I know exactly how he felt about this place. He's probably turning over in his grave just hearing your suggestions.''

''You're the most stubborn, irritating man I've ever met.''

Zach laughed bitterly. "If what your father said was true, I'm probably the only *man* you've ever met."

"I beg your pardon," she said in indignation. "Just what is that supposed to mean? How would my father know anything about the men I associate with?"

"Your father visited you at some yacht club a few months before he died," Zach said as he flipped the flapjacks with the flair of an experienced cook. "To put it mildly, he was very disappointed with your choice of friends, lady. Said they were all spoiled, rich wimps."

"He had a lot of nerve," Charlene hissed. "And why didn't he approach me and tell me who he was?"

"Unfortunately the tumor produced several symptoms that would come and go in the early stages of his illness. One was lapse of memory, one was a trembling in his hand. From what he told me, both symptoms hit him hard the night he planned to talk to you. He was afraid he was going to die alone in San Francisco, so he came home before he had a chance to talk to you."

Charlene was silent.

"Do you want maple syrup or strawberry preserves?" Zach asked as he set their plates on the table.

"What? Oh . . . whatever. He had planned to talk to me?" she asked, still thinking about her father being in San Francisco.

"He went right from the hospital in Houston to San Francisco to see you and your mother," Zach explained, putting a big jug of maple syrup on the table. "He wanted to try to make amends before he died."

"If he was this decent man you say he was, why didn't he try to do that earlier?"

"He did. Your grandmother wouldn't let him," he answered as he spread butter on his flapjacks. "Dig in before they get cold," he suggested.

"I don't believe your story, Mr. Leighton," she said as she buttered her flapjacks.

"Fine," he answered, taking a bite of sausage. "No skin off my nose."

Charlene took a bite, then another. "Ummm, these are really very good," she said, surprise in her voice.

"I told you they would be. I could teach you to make a western omelet that would knock your socks off."

"What an exciting prospect," she said sarcastically. After another few bites she stared across the table at him. "You really don't plan to sell to me, do you?"

"Nope. This ranch is my life. You couldn't care less about it."

"You're right about that. Not in its present state anyway," she admitted.

"Have you ever heard the expression, 'stop and smell the roses'?" Zach asked.

"Of course," she answered, annoyance in her voice.

"It means to enjoy nature, Lady Van Payton. Have you ever done that? Have you ever sat on a mountaintop and just stared at the clouds, or sat in a field of wildflowers and listened to the buzzing of insects around you, or fished in a clear, unpolluted stream or river, and then pan-fried the fish on the spot?''

''Of course not. I have more important things to do,'' she answered defensively.

''Yeah, like drinking at the yacht club with your worthless friends, or shopping for a fur coat without regard to the living things that had to be killed so you could wear it. No, you don't know how to live, lady, and apparently you don't want to know how, or you wouldn't be talking about changing this place.''

''Oh, I suppose you consider being isolated on this mountain living?''

''You bet I do,'' he answered angrily. ''You learn about the seasons of life and the seasons of your own soul. You learn about yourself, the good and the bad, and you learn to live and appreciate both sides. You could stand to do a little soul-searching, lady.''

''I hate to burst your bubble, Mr. Leighton, but I'm very content with myself and my life. You're the one who lives here like a hermit. Could that possibly be because no one could live with you?'' she asked smugly.

Zach glared across the table at her. ''I live here because it's one of the few places where I don't have to put up with humans who want to destroy everything they touch for the almighty dollar. We don't own the earth. It is only loaned to us, and if we don't start taking care of every mountain, every seashore, every meadow, we'll end up destroying it and ourselves.''

''Oh, please,'' Charlene exclaimed. ''You sound like some TV preacher trying to make people believe.''

''And what do you believe in, Lady Van Payton?''

''I believe in success,'' she answered smugly.

"And the almighty dollar," Zach said in disgust. "Just as I thought."

"That, too," she admitted. "As I said, you have an attitude problem, Mr. Leighton. You think your way is the only way. You need to get off this mountain and get a life—or at least experience life with someone other than the wildlife you seem to favor."

"No thanks," he said, pushing away from the table. "From what I've seen of your kind, I prefer the wildlife." He pulled on his coat. "While you clean up the kitchen I'll check out the cabins."

Charlene watched him go out the kitchen door. "I'm not your maid," she mumbled as she cleared the dishes off the table. *I can see I'm not going to get anyplace with Mr. Zach Leighton,* she thought as she ran water over the sticky dishes. *I may as well get out of this place and let my lawyers handle him.* Maybe she could still get back in time for Zelda's party on Friday night, she thought as she dropped the dishes into the sink. "You can do your own dishes, Mr. Mountain Man. I'm going back to San Francisco."

Dressed in her designer jeans, high-heel boots, and fur coat, Charlene headed for the jeep, dragging her bags behind her. "Damn," she hissed, slipping and sliding in the snow. "Why would anyone want to live under these conditions? Oh, no," she exclaimed, spotting the jeep buried in the snow. Dropping her bags, she circled the vehicle, trying to decide how to go about cleaning the snow away. "Where is a man when you need one?"

After twenty minutes of trying to clear the snow away with her hands, Charlene went in search of

Zach Leighton. She found him clearing a path to the line of cabins.

"Mr. Leighton," she called out. "I have decided to leave and let you and my lawyer discuss this property. If you'd like to be rid of me, would you mind helping me get my jeep out of the snow."

When Zach didn't answer, she continued with her pitch, trying to keep her voice light and pleasant. "I suppose I could wait until later today and let the sun melt the snow, but I'd really like to be on my way now. I have a party I'd like to attend on Friday . . ."

"A party? Good heavens, we wouldn't want to miss a party now, would we?" he said with a sarcastic laugh.

Zach continued what he was doing, making Charlene furious. "Mr. Leighton, surely that path to the cabins can wait to be shoveled another time. There isn't anyone staying in them, so what difference does a little snow make? I don't think I'm being unreasonable asking for your help. It isn't like you have anything important to do," she continued, her voice getting higher and higher, while he ignored her. Suddenly she screamed at him. "Will you stop what you're doing and help me, or shall I call AAA?"

Zach threw down his shovel. "Damnit, woman, you really are a pain in the . . ." he let the last word fade. "You haven't listened to anything I've said," he shouted. "This is Wyoming. When the snow starts here it doesn't stop until spring, and it sure as hell doesn't melt overnight. If it isn't cleaned off the roofs, they will collapse, if the water pipes aren't checked daily, they can freeze, and if we run out of wood or let the fire in the lodge go out, we could have a real problem with frozen pipes and be without running water for the entire winter, and *Lady*,'' he drawled, ''AAA isn't going to come up the mountain to your rescue, nor is that four-wheel-drive vehicle going to get you off this mountain. You may as well make the best of it because you're going to be here a while, and you're going to do things my way.''

Charlene stared at him dumbfounded. ''You are the rudest, most hardheaded man I've ever met, and I detest you and this terrible place,'' she swore venomously. ''This backwoods, macho man routine may work on the people around here, but not on me, Zach Leighton. I don't need your help. I'll call AAA myself,'' she said, turning on her heels and heading for the lodge in a huff.

''You do that,'' he shouted after her. ''Then start studying one of those cookbooks, because I'm not going to be your cook and servant while you're here!''

SIX

Two hours later Zach entered the lodge and found Charlene sitting in front of the fireplace, staring into the flames with an open magazine on her lap. "I thought AAA was coming for you."

"You knew very well they wouldn't," she snapped, "and I don't need to hear any more of your sarcastic remarks. I'm trying my best to get off this mountain and leave you alone. I even called my mother to see if the Van Payton helicopter could come for me, but it's on loan to Senator Smith for the next thirty days, which infuriates me," she said, tossing the magazine aside. "I just don't understand it at all."

He could hear the emotion in her voice and knew she was struggling to hold back the tears.

"What don't you understand?" Zach asked, almost feeling sorry for her.

"I can never remember my grandmother or mother lending Van Payton aircraft to anyone."

"I suppose there is a first time for everything,

even for a Van Payton to be generous,'' Zach commented as he poured himself a cup of coffee.

''You know nothing about the Van Paytons,'' she said defensively. ''My family's generosity is well known all over California.''

''And all tax deductible.''

''You're so self-righteous and boring,'' she spat. ''It's no wonder you live alone. No one could stand to live with you.''

''You said that before, ma'am,'' he agreed, ''and unfortunately you're about to find out for yourself just how boring I can be, because you're going to be here for a while.''

''Not if I can help it,'' she retorted.

''I'm going to have a cheese sandwich and a beer,'' Zach said calmly, as if they weren't in the middle of an argument. ''Do you want to join me?''

Charlene watched him head for the kitchen, furious that he wasn't going to argue with her. She needed some way to vent her frustration. She followed him, realizing what he had offered. A cheese sandwich. Cheese was used as a sauce over broccoli or asparagus, but a sandwich . . .

''Do you want mayonnaise or mustard?'' he asked as she entered the kitchen.

''Whatever you're having. I would prefer a glass of white wine instead of a beer, though.''

''I just bet you would, but beer and soft drinks are all I have, unless you want to make tea or coffee.''

Charlene sighed as she sat at the wooden table. ''Beer will be fine.''

Zach set the sandwich in front of her. ''How about a sour pickle? It goes real good with a cheese sandwich.''

"Whatever you say. I know nothing about cheese sandwiches, or what goes with them," she sighed.

"You've got a lot to learn, Lady Van Payton. I think you're going to find that you've missed out on a lot of good things."

"Oh, please. Now you're going to try to convince me that a cheese sandwich rates up there with caviar or lobster?"

"Maybe not lobster, but it sure beats eating fish eggs," he said with a laugh.

She was surprised how quickly his mood had changed. Just a few minutes ago he had been her adversary, and now suddenly he was being very pleasant. "I suppose caviar is an acquired taste," she admitted, taking a bite of her sandwich. Zach set an open bottle of beer in front of her. "I'd like a glass, if you don't mind."

"Shucks, ma'am, I don't mind a bit, as long as you're washing dishes. They're in the cupboard right behind you."

Charlene didn't comment on the dishes as she got up to get a glass. She wondered if he had noticed the breakfast dishes still in the sink. She took another couple of bites before speaking again. "Mr. Leighton, what do you think my chances are of getting off this mountain today, or tomorrow at the latest?"

Zach took another bite of his sandwich, then shrugged his shoulders. "Slim to none."

"I can't believe this," she stated in exasperation. "I only have enough cigarettes to last me until tomorrow."

"I tried to warn you yesterday," he said congenially.

Charlene took a drink of her beer. "Yes, but I thought you were just trying to get rid of me."

"I was, because I know the weather around here. Even if you got off this mountain, there is a good chance the airport would be closed. I keep telling you this isn't San Francisco."

"That's an understatement, Mr. Leighton," she sighed. She studied him as he finished his sandwich. He wasn't too bad-looking, she thought. The dark hair and light blue eyes were an arresting contrast, and he was certainly built adequately. It was a shame he was such a backwoods hick. She had to admit, though, he was charismatic, in a different, rugged way.

"Is there something on my face?" he asked, a grin touching the corner of his mouth.

"What? Oh, no. I'm sorry, I was . . ." She glanced around the kitchen. "I was just thinking that at least the kitchen is pretty well equipped. I would bring in a restaurant-size freezer and refrigerator, though."

"Won't do any good if the power goes out, which it often does."

"What in the world do you do then?"

"Bury the food in the snow and hope like hell the animals don't eat it. You can get mighty tired of eating fish for months on end."

"How can you stand to live like this?" she asked in disbelief.

"Like what?" he asked, pretending not to understand her.

"Like a . . . like an Eskimo" was all she could think of to compare it to.

"It might get cold in here, ma'am, but this isn't an igloo."

"You know what I mean, Mr. Leighton. Just think

about it. You could sell out to me and go live someplace like San Francisco or New York."

"What a terrible thought, ma'am. Why, I'd be as out of place in a city as a nun in a whorehouse."

Charlene shook her head at his rustic phrasing. He must never have been off this mountain, she thought to herself. "You may have a point, Mr. Leighton, but you could always go to school and learn a trade. Perhaps then you'd fit in."

"Don't think so, ma'am," he said with a smile before taking a swig of his beer. He was tempted to inform her that he had a degree in environmental engineering and a degree in forestry, but he decided it was more fun letting her think he was an uneducated buffoon. She was amusing, he'd have to give her that. He'd never met anyone quite so naive. Her mother and grandmother did a good job keeping her isolated from the real world.

"Since you're going to be here for a while, I think we need to set down some rules. As I said before, you're going to have to share the chores."

"Chores?" Charlene repeated, her green eyes wide.

"Yes, ma'am. Chores like cooking, cleaning, and splitting wood. But don't worry, little lady, I'll take care of the wood splitting. That's man's work."

"How kind of you, Mr. Leighton," Charlene said, getting to her feet, "but I haven't given up on getting my jeep out of the snow yet."

"Whatever you say, ma'am. There's a shovel right next to the back door, but don't you go hurting yourself now," he drawled.

Charlene gave him a mutinous glare before leaving the kitchen. "The man is a hayseed," she mumbled to herself as she slipped into her fur coat. "Nun in a whorehouse . . . Where does he come up with these things?"

Zach put a couple of logs on the fire and settled down on the sofa with a book, waiting for Lady Van Payton to see that her ambitious task was impossible. Half an hour later, he put the book aside, unable to concentrate. He wandered to the window, telling himself he didn't care what the woman did, yet a nagging voice reminded him how cold it was, and the stupid woman didn't even have waterproof boots or a hat. If he thought she had a chance of getting off this mountain he'd help her dig that antiquated jeep out, but Hawk's Cry was over seven miles from any main road—seven miles of snow banks and mountains with snowdrifts just waiting to crash down on the roads at the slightest sound.

He watched her pause, wiping her hands on her expensive fur coat. "It's probably the first physical work the woman has ever done," he mumbled to himself as he poured a cup of coffee. Maybe she'd tire herself out and give him a little peace this evening.

Charlene worked for over an hour before finally deciding she'd have to finish her job in the morning. She was physically exhausted and freezing, but she had cleared the snow away from the front end of the jeep and was proud of her accomplishment.

Zach looked up from his book when she entered the lodge. She was white as a ghost, and her lips were blue. Her fancy coat looked like she had been swimming in it. "Want some coffee?" he asked.

Charlene was surprised and relieved that he hadn't made some cutting remark. She was too tired to argue any more this evening. "Coffee would be wonderful, but I'm going to take a hot shower first."

"I thought you might want to do that. I turned on a heater in the bathroom and put a flannel robe on the back of the door. It's one I found in a cabin," he explained, not wanting to sound like he was getting soft about her being there.

"Thank you," she said, wondering what he was up to. "I won't be but a minute."

"Good, because we have to decide what to fix for dinner—together," he added for good measure. "And I'm starved."

"Oh . . ." Charlene fumed as she headed for the bathroom. She should have known he couldn't be nice for more than a minute. Here she was exhausted while he sat in a warm house, reading a book. Now he wanted her to help fix dinner. She had heard of chauvinistic men, but this one had to be the worst.

Zach smiled to himself as he took a frying chicken from the refrigerator. She sure was easy to aggravate. It certainly wasn't going to be boring having her around.

Since Zach Leighton had told her to hurry, Charlene decided to take a leisurely shower. She washed her hair, then let the hot water run over her tired, aching muscles. She couldn't understand the man. He considerately put a heater on, offered her coffee, then abruptly tells her to hurry up so she could fix dinner. He had a lot of nerve, but she'd show him she wasn't going to be bossed around.

When Charlene came out of the bathroom she could smell something delicious cooking. Wrapping the robe tightly around her, her hair still bound in a towel, she entered the kitchen. Chicken was frying, potatoes were boiling, and Zach was dipping some green vegetable in corn meal. "Smells wonderful," she commented, perching herself on the stool at the counter.

"Fried chicken, mashed potatoes, and fried okra," he announced. "I couldn't wait for you, so you got clean-up duty again."

"Fine," she agreed. She'd clean up a few dishes for some good food, and this definitely smelled good.

Zach tried to keep his eyes on what he was doing, but she looked mighty appealing in the flannel robe with her hair wrapped in a towel. He kept waiting for the damned thing to fall open. God, he had been on this mountain too long, he decided. How could he possibly find this selfish woman appealing? "Ready for that coffee?" he asked.

"Yes, but I can get it," she said, slipping from the stool.

Zach glanced down at her bare feet. "Don't you have socks or slippers to put on your feet?"

"Only my wet boots, or a pair of high heels."

Zach left the kitchen and came back a moment later with a pair of heavy socks. "Here, put these on. They'll help some."

"Thanks," she said, slipping the socks over her cold feet. "I got half the jeep dug out, so I should be able to get out of your hair by tomorrow."

"You think so?" he said as he placed the fried chicken on a paper towel. "Why don't we fix our plates and eat in front of the fireplace?"

"Sounds wonderful," Charlene agreed. "I don't

think I'll ever be warm again. The cold penetrated to my bones."

After dinner, Zach played his guitar while Charlene washed dishes. When she joined him on the couch, he was playing an upbeat country tune.

"Can you play anything besides country music?" she asked.

"Sure," he smiled, breaking into Ted Nugent's "Cat Scratch Fever," a raunchy rock tune.

"That wasn't what I had in mind," she said, pulling her feet up under her. "I enjoy opera and classical music."

"Never learned to play opera," he said with a grin, "but if you have any other requests."

"Anything is fine," she said, twirling a cigarette between her hands.

Zach studied her, thinking how long her ink-black lashes were. They were a beautiful contrast to her blond hair.

"Is that your last one?" he asked.

"Yes. I'm trying to save it for tomorrow morning, but I need one bad."

"Good time to give up the nasty habit," he commented as he strummed the guitar.

"You make it sound so easy," she snapped. "I suppose you have never smoked?"

"As a matter of fact, I kicked the habit a few years ago, and I've never felt better."

"Hooray for you," she said sarcastically. "I think I'm going to turn in. I'm exhausted. Would you wake me early so I can start on the jeep?"

Zach smiled. "Be glad to, Lady Van Payton. You

sleep good now, you hear, and don't let the bed bugs bite."

Charlene moaned and pulled the cover over her head. She just had to get the jeep out of the snow in the morning or she'd surely go crazy isolated on this mountain with a hayseed—and no cigarettes.

SEVEN

Zach had just dozed off when Charlene let out a blood-curdling scream. He was on his feet, ready to do battle with an intruder, when he realized the sound of a wolf's lonesome howl was what had frightened her. "It's all right," he assured her, sitting on the side of her bed.

Charlene wrapped her arms around his waist and clung to him. "Please don't leave me. There's something terrible out there."

He ran his hand up and down her arm in a comforting gesture. "It's only a wolf, and he's miles away," he whispered to her.

"Why is it making that sound? It sounds so sad," she whispered.

Again the silence of the night was broken by the string of hauntingly soulful cries of the wolves harmonizing with each other.

"They're reaffirming the pack's ties," Zach explained as he stroked her silky hair. "Sometimes they can be heard six miles away. Many believe their howl is their way of building territorial fences for their pack.''

"They sound so eerie," Charlene whispered, still clinging tightly to Zach.

"The Indians felt there was a mystical quality about the wolf, and regarded him as a conduit between the realms of spirit and earth."

"I can understand why. They sound like something from another world," she said with a shiver.

"You'll get used to it," Zach assured. "Your father used to love to hear them. He called their howls a moonlight sonata, and he'd sit outside for hours listening to them."

"It makes me feel sad and alone," she admitted softly.

"You're not alone," he asserted, letting the scent of her delicate perfume wash over him. "I'm right here with you until you're ready to go back to sleep."

"Would you please turn a light on? It's terribly dark in here."

"Are you planning to be awake the rest of the night?" he asked.

"No, but I'd really prefer a light on. I don't like the dark."

Zach laughed. "I'm not going to attack you, if that's what you're worried about. I was just trying to comfort you."

"No . . . it isn't that. I know it's probably ridiculous, but I never have liked the dark. It always made being alone more . . . more intense. At home I always sleep with a light on. My grandmother used to get very annoyed with me. She said that I should be above being afraid of anything."

Zach's arms tightened around her. "Everyone is afraid of something. I'm sure your grandmother had some hang-ups."

Charlene laughed bitterly. "You didn't know my grandmother. She taught me never to show feelings. I was also taught never to trust feelings. Always use my mind, not my emotions, she said."

"As I said, your grandmother had some hang-ups," Zach said, pulling her closer. Charlene Van Payton tried to act cool and grown up, but in many ways she was still a little girl needing love, companionship, and protection. If only Cody had had a chance to know and help his daughter.

"The light . . ." she reminded him, bringing him out of his thoughts.

Zach leaned over and turned the light on. "Would you like me to hold you for a while longer?"

Charlene was silent for a long moment, then she answered in a soft whisper. "I wouldn't mind."

Zach could feel her stiffen when his hand touched the underside of her breast. He wanted her to relax, not be frightened of him, so he decided to try some conversation.

"What do you do for enjoyment when you're in San Francisco?"

"Enjoyment?" she asked, her voice sounding bewildered. "I . . . I like to sail and play golf."

"I've never tried either, but always thought I would like to someday," he commented as he ran his hand up and down her arm in a comforting gesture.

"What do *you* like to do?" Charlene asked softly, still clinging to him.

"In the summer I enjoy riding up into the mountains and camping."

"I haven't seen any horses here. I thought this was supposed to be a dude ranch?"

Zach laughed softly. "It is. The horses have been sent to Riverton for the winter. It gets too harsh up here for them."

"So not even the beasts can stand it," Charlene said, stifling a yawn.

"Am I keeping you awake?"

"No," she answered, snuggling closer to him. She felt safe and secure in his arms, a feeling she had never felt with a man before, and she didn't want it to end just yet. "What do you enjoy doing in the winter?"

"I enjoy cross-country skiing and snowmobiling."

"Snowmobiling sounds like fun."

"If you're here for a while I'll teach you to do both."

Charlene yawned again. "I saw a television special on people snowmobiling in upstate New York."

Zach had to smile. "Is this your first time away from San Francisco?"

"Certainly not," she answered indignantly. "I've been to New York several times, and to Washington, D.C., and I was supposed to go to Europe when I finished school, but my grandmother died and I've been too busy since to go."

"What have you been busy with?" Zach asked.

"Mother wants me to take over the resort properties division of Van Payton Enterprises, and I've been working with the manager of the department to learn everything about it."

"Is that what you want to do?"

"Of course. What else would I do?"

"I don't know," he mused. "You're tall and slender, and I suppose some would say beautiful. You could be a model or an actress."

Charlene giggled. "As a matter of fact, Mr. Leighton, I was approached by a modeling agency, but Van Payton women are expected to join the business."

"Following tradition, eh? Don't all Van Payton women also end up single and alone?"

"That's not a prerequisite," she answered defensively. "It's just a coincidence that my grandmother was widowed at a very young age and that my mother divorced at a young age."

"I certainly agree with you. Women in power don't have to lose their sensitivity, or their need to be loved. Do you have anyone special in your life?" he asked when the silence drew out for long awkward moments.

"No," she admitted softly. "I have friends I go places with, but I'm not serious about any of them."

"Cody would be pleased to hear that. He didn't think much of the friends he saw you with at your yacht club."

Charlene sat up and glared at Zach. "Mr. Leighton, I don't care what you say, I don't believe for a moment that Cody Jones cared a whit about me, or what I did. If he had, he would have visited me when I was a child."

"I keep telling you he tried, but your grandmother wouldn't allow it."

"I don't believe that," she said, tears welling up in her lovely green eyes. "My grandmother would never have done anything to hurt me."

"When you get back to San Francisco why don't you ask your mother about it?" he suggested.

"I intend to do just that."

"Lie back down and relax," he encouraged, missing the warmth of her in his arms.

When she did as he asked, he began to stroke her soft, silky hair.

"You haven't told me if you have anyone special in your life?" she commented.

"Well, there is a bear that comes around, and a beautiful doe, and that wolf that you heard . . ."

Charlene laughed. "I don't doubt any of that, but I'm talking about two-legged creatures."

Zach laughed. Suddenly and unexplainably they were congenial companions. "You'll have to call me Zach if I'm going to tell you my life story."

"And you'll really have to stop calling me Lady Van Payton and call me Charlene," she said with a yawn. "Does Zach stand for Zachariah?"

"You got it, and I don't want to hear any derogatory comments about it."

"I wasn't going to say anything about it. As a matter of fact, I like it. It has a nice sound. Zachariah," she repeated, letting it roll off her tongue.

Suddenly Charlene sat up and stared at him. "I just realized something. For the last thirty minutes we have been talking and not once have you sounded like an uneducated mountain man."

Zach laughed. "Maybe that's because I'm not one."

"What do you mean?" she asked, confused.

"I've been to college, Charlene. I have a degree in forestry, and a master's degree in environmental engineering. I've traveled in Europe and worked in

Washington, D.C., on environmental issues. I wasn't born on this mountain, but it's where I hope to live and raise a family."

"Why did you let me think you were . . . were . . ." She stuttered over her words.

"Stupid," he filled in for her. "It's what you wanted to believe, so I thought I'd humor you."

For a moment Charlene was angry that he had duped her, then she laughed. "You're a very strange man, Zachariah Leighton. I should be angry with you, but I'm too tired."

"Good. Why don't you close your eyes and get some sleep?"

She snuggled back into his arms. "You haven't told me about yourself yet."

"We'll save that for tomorrow night," he said, pulling the covers up under her chin.

"I don't plan to be here tomorrow night, Mr . . . Zachariah."

"I know you don't, Charley. Go to sleep now. I'll leave the light on for you."

She closed her eyes and smiled. Charley, he had called her. She liked that. When she was here in his arms she felt like a Charley, not the Charlene who lived in San Francisco in a big mansion with all her servants—and her loneliness.

EIGHT

The tension between them seemed to have eased, and making breakfast the next morning turned out to be a pleasant situation for a change.

Charlene carefully laid strips of bacon in the iron skillet. "How's that?" she asked as Zach fixed a pot of coffee.

"Fine," he said, trying to keep a straight face, "but I'd suggest you turn the flame on under the pan."

"Oh, darn," she said in frustration. "There are just too many things to remember."

"You did fine mixing the biscuits," he encouraged.

"I had a book instructing me in every step," she said with a sigh.

"True, but not everyone can follow the instructions in a cookbook."

Charlene laughed. "Thank you. That makes me feel a little better, but it still doesn't mean I'm going to be your cook. I plan to dig the rest of the snow away from the jeep this morning and then hopefully be on my way."

"Have you looked out the window this morning?" he asked as he broke eggs into the skillet.

"No. Why? Did the snow melt?" she asked hopefully.

"Not exactly. Over easy all right with you?"

"Fine," she answered, heading for the window. "Oh, no!"

"Looks to me like another foot," Zach commented.

"After all my work," she said dishearteningly. "Well, I'll just have to start all over after breakfast."

"Good for you," Zach said as he slipped two eggs onto her plate. "Determination is half the battle."

"Do I detect a hint of sarcasm in that remark?"

Zach smiled. "Charley, if I thought you had a chance of getting off this mountain, I'd help you, but I don't, so why don't you just relax and enjoy your stay."

"I have one cigarette left to have with my coffee, so I have to get off this mountain this morning," she insisted. "Besides, the only reason you want me to stay is so I can cook for you."

Zach took a bite of his food. "That isn't really true. I said if you stayed you'd have to help, which is only fair. Besides, I had the feeling you enjoyed making biscuits this morning."

"I did, but that doesn't mean I want to stay here just so I can learn to cook."

"Learning to cook would be a bonus. I thought you might like to stay and learn a little about your father and his world."

Charlene took a bite of her egg before answering. "I don't know what made you think that."

Zach shrugged. "I thought you mellowed about that subject a little last night."

"You were mistaken. These biscuits are really very good," she said, changing the subject. "If I wanted to, I imagine I could be an excellent cook."

Zach laughed. "That's what I like. Beauty and modesty, too."

Charlene smiled as she ate. That was the second time he had mentioned that he thought she was beautiful. It might even be pleasant spending a few days with him. It had felt so good being held in his strong arms last night, but damn, she needed to get some cigarettes.

"Do you think it's possible a guest could have left some cigarettes behind in one of the cabins?" she asked.

"The cabins were thoroughly cleaned before the crew left. I'm sure if any had been left behind they would have been thrown out or taken by the crew. Why don't you just kick the nasty habit? It's a perfect opportunity. This mountain is a perfect place to change your way of thinking, your life-style, and any bad habits you might have."

Charlene rolled her eyes heavenward. "You didn't mention last night that you were also a preacher."

"Sorry. I didn't mean to preach. I just hate to see a beautiful woman ruining her health by smoking."

Suddenly Charlene got to her feet. "I don't want to hear it, Zach. I've been told all my life what I should and shouldn't do, and the more people tell me what to do, the more I do what I want. So leave me alone!" she shouted.

Zach smiled. "Already feeling that nicotine withdrawal, eh? Well, don't worry about it. I can put up with your mood swings for a few days if you can."

"Damn it, Zach Leighton, stop patronizing me. I need a cigarette."

"How about another cup of coffee instead?"

"No. I'm going to dig the jeep out."

Zach finished his coffee and then went to check on the cabins. He cleared his path, then began checking water pipes. The wind was picking up and he knew the snow would be drifting again. Tomorrow he'd probably have to clear the snow off the roofs or they'd be collapsing under the weight. He found his mind wandering to Charlene and what they could do later. Perhaps she'd enjoy fishing with him after lunch. He could teach her to cut a hole in the ice and fish through it. It was strange, he had thought he wanted to spend his winter alone, isolated from the world, yet he had to admit, since last night he began to think it might be pleasant to have her around for a while. She had seemed like a frightened little girl. Hell, he thought as he started back to the lodge. Maybe that was the reason for her behavior. She was probably just a scared kid in a woman's body. It didn't sound like anyone back in San Francisco cared a damn for her.

Suddenly he heard the jeep motor start. He had a feeling of panic as he rushed up the path. Surely she hadn't been able to get that damned jeep out of the snow. When he turned the corner of the last cabin he saw the jeep break through the snow and begin to move forward.

"No!" he shouted, running toward her. "Damnit, woman, stop!" The snow was nearly three feet deep, and deeper where it had drifted. Even though the jeep was moving slowly, he was having trouble making progress.

"Fool woman," he shouted as the jeep widened the space between them. He stopped, gulping deep breaths of air, trying to decide what to do as he watched the jeep disappear around the bend. She'd never make it. There was no way to distinguish the road in this heavy a snow. She'd end up going off . . . Oh, God, he had to do something.

Suddenly he turned around and ran toward the stables where he kept a snowmobile. It wasn't much good in drifting snow, but it was all he had, other than his pickup, and he knew that wasn't going anyplace in this deep snow.

Charlene bounced and careened through the snow, straining to see ahead of her. The wind was blowing the snow, obscuring her vision. It was all she could do to keep the wheel in her cold hands, but she forged ahead. Wouldn't Zach be surprised when she showed him that it wasn't impossible to get off the mountain? She'd have to drop him a note, or maybe call him when she got back to San Francisco—ask him to send her belongings to her.

The bitter cold air whipped around her, and her feet felt as if they were frozen chunks of ice. Damn, if she could just get some heat out of this decrepit old piece of machinery, she thought. Suddenly she hit a deep snowbank and the jeep bucked and slid sideways. "Come on, Bessie," she pleaded, knowing that if she got stuck now she'd really be in trouble. She had to keep her bearings, she knew, remembering the deep gorges that the road wound through.

Oh, God, maybe she should turn around and go

back, she thought when she couldn't see the road anymore. She shifted gears and gently touched the brakes, but it was too late. The jeep began to slide sideways, and before she knew it she was rolling down an embankment, over and over, as if in slow motion. She screamed as she was thrown from one side of the jeep to the other, until finally the jeep came to a stop. "Oh, God," she moaned in pain. All she could see was blackness. She was engulfed in snow, sealed in an icy cocoon.

She tried to concentrate on breathing, but the snow packed around her seemed to squeeze the breath from her chest. She had no idea how deeply she was buried, or even which way was up. She couldn't move her legs and only one arm had enough space to wiggle, but with that arm she struggled to move snow away from her face. Finally, exhausted, she gave up, knowing she wasn't going to break out of her cold, icy prison. Melted snow from her breath formed a glaze of ice inches from her face, a mask of death that was sealing off her oxygen.

She began to shiver violently. *This is it,* she thought. *I'm going to die here and they won't find my body until spring. Oh, God, why didn't I listen to Zach? Why haven't I ever listened to anyone? He won't even know I didn't make it—until the snow melts.*

God, she felt so sleepy. Why couldn't she keep her eyes open? Time seemed frozen, along with everything else, she thought dreamily. She wondered if the gang at the yacht club would have a good laugh about the way she had died. Charlene Van Payton, who always traveled in a chauffeured limousine, dying in a beat-up World War II jeep, she thought as she drifted in and out of sleep. She thought of her mother, and wished they had been closer. She knew her mother had always been lonely. Maybe that was why she had spent every waking moment buried in her work. Why hadn't she insisted they spend more time together, instead of always running off to join her friends? Her worthless friends, she thought. Cody Jones had been right about that. They had all been born to money and had no ambition to do anything but spend it, and she was the same way. What had she accomplished that she could be proud of? Nothing! Her epitaph would read: Charlene Van Payton, rich, spoiled, worthless daughter of Emily Van Payton. Oh, God, why hadn't she realized how she was wasting her life? If she had a chance to do it over again, it would be different. She wouldn't have let her grandmother send her away to school when she didn't want to go away from home. She knew her mother hadn't wanted her to go, but neither of them had been any match for Agatha Van Payton. Her grandmother insisted that every young lady of breeding had to attend a finishing school. Those had been such lonely years. If her father had been around maybe he would have stood up to her grandmother. "Stop it, Charlene. You're out of your head."

Had her grandmother really ruined her mother and father's marriage? she wondered as she dozed in and out of consciousness. She wouldn't put it past her to do anything to get what she wanted. Even though her grandmother doted on her, giving her every material thing she could want, she was known as a very ruthless woman in the business world.

"Who's there?" she mumbled, thinking she heard

a man's voice telling her to hang on. Oh, God, she was delirious, she thought. There wasn't anyone within miles of her. There was the voice again. The end must be near, she thought, resigned to the fact.

Suddenly Charlene forced her eyes open. She thought she heard the hum of a motor. For a moment she felt hope, but then she realized it was unlikely anyone would be able to see the jeep, even if they were out looking for her. She knew she had rolled over at least six times, so she was probably deep in some gorge. "I'm sorry I didn't listen to you, Zach," she whispered, "and I'm sorry I didn't get to know you better . . ."

Her last thought was of a psalm one of her nannies used to recite to her at bedtime when she was a little girl: "I lift up my eyes to the hills. From whence does my help come? My help comes from the Lord, who made heaven and earth."

NINE

"Come on, princess, cooperate," Zach encouraged, trying to work the frozen boots off her feet.

"Am I dead?" she asked in a hoarse voice.

"No, but we've got to get your body temperature up, and I've got to get these wet things off you. I'm going to have to cut your boots away."

"So cold . . ." she mumbled. "Want to sleep . . ."

"I know you're cold, and I'm going to try to do something about it, but you have to stay awake. Come on now, honey, I need your help. We have to do this together."

Zach was concerned at her coloring. The blue of her lips was a frightening contrast with the gray of her skin. He had to keep her awake and get her moving. "I've got some long johns and wool socks I want to get on you, and then we're going to take a stroll in front of the fireplace to get your circulation back."

"Fire," she mumbled as he finally worked her boots off. "So cold."

Zach shook his head when he discovered she only had stockings on under the boots. ''Damn fool woman,'' he mumbled. She was going to be lucky if she didn't lose her toes. He worked her tight, wet designer jeans down her legs. She was shivering and her chattering teeth sounded like castanets. ''It won't be long now,'' he assured her. ''Raise your bottom.''

''What are you doing?'' she asked, grabbing at her panty hose as he began to lower them.

''Sorry, sweetheart, but we're going to have to be on very intimate terms for a while. There is no other way,'' he said, placing a blanket over her lower body as he stripped the last remaining garment off. He held up a pair of black lace panties. ''Very nice,'' he said, ''but once I get you into these warm long johns, I bet you'll be a lot more comfortable.''

She feebly protested as he removed her sweater and bra and began rubbing her down briskly with a thick terry towel. Her skin felt like ice to his hands. ''OK, princess, take another drink of this coffee and then we'll get you dressed and up.''

Charlene swallowed as he held the cup to her lips. ''Don't want to get up. Want to sleep.''

''No way, Charley. You've got some walking to do,'' he insisted as he slipped the heavy wool socks on her feet, then began inching the long johns up her body. After rolling the excess material on the legs and sleeves, he put a pair of oversize Indian moccasins on her feet. ''Here we go,'' he said, lifting her to her feet. ''Move your feet,'' he ordered. ''It won't help your circulation if I have to carry you.''

''Please, I'm so tired. Can't I just rest?''

''I know you're tired,'' he said sympathetically,

"but we have to do this. I'll let you sleep as soon as we get your body temperature up." Zach pulled her against him and moved toward the fire. "Come on, move your feet, Charlene. They'll feel better in no time," he assured, trying to keep the concern from his voice. They paced the room over and over, with him giving words of encouragement the whole time. He picked up the mug of coffee and held it to her lips. "Drink a little more."

"Please, can we rest now?" she asked after sipping the hot liquid. "My legs feel like lead."

"Just a little more walking, then I'll check your feet. How do your hands feel?"

"Still a little numb and tingling, but better."

"Good. That's progress. You're mighty lucky I found you when I did."

"How *did* you find me? I thought I was buried under the snow."

"You were, all except for one tire that showed through. I followed your tracks and saw that you'd gone over the edge. After that it was just a matter of digging you out. You're damned lucky. If that tire hadn't been exposed I might not have found you. People have been lost in these mountains during a storm and never found."

Charlene yawned, yet the seriousness of his words hit home. She knew very well how lucky she was. She couldn't believe that she was here with him now. Only a few hours ago she'd given up the fight, certain she was going to die.

"How come you didn't let me die? If I had, you wouldn't have to worry about having a partner."

"Umm, I didn't think about that," he said, amusement in his voice. "All I kept thinking about was losing my cook."

She stumbled against him. "Can't walk much more . . ."

"All right. Sit down on the side of the bed and let me feel your feet."

Charlene sank down and slowly fell over backward. "So sleepy."

Zach removed her slippers and socks and felt her feet. "Oh, God," she cried out. "They hurt . . ."

"That's a good sign. It means the feeling is coming back. They will probably hurt like hell for a while, but at least your body temperature is coming up."

"That's comforting," she mumbled. "I'm going to hurt like hell for a while, but you think that's a good sign."

Zach had to laugh. "You're mighty lucky, lady. I wouldn't complain about anything if I were you. And I hope the hell you'll think twice before you wear high heel boots out in the snow again. They're no protection against anything."

"They cost me four hundred dollars," she protested feebly.

"I don't care if they cost a thousand dollars. They're not appropriate for snow, or even walking, but that's beside the point now, because they're ruined. I had to cut them off of you. I'll have to see if one of the wranglers left something behind that you can wear."

"What's a wrangler?" she asked as she snuggled down under the quilts.

"I'll tell you tomorrow. Go ahead and sleep now." When she didn't say anything he realized she had already dozed off. "You had a guardian angel today, princess, that's for sure."

Zach headed for the kitchen and got a beer and some cheese and crackers. He hadn't had anything to eat since breakfast and he was suddenly starved. God, it had seemed like a long day. He was just relieved it had turned out the way it had. If he hadn't gotten to the girl when he did she would surely have died. As it was, he was still worrying about frostbite.

He took a drink of his beer and thought about what had happened. He had made finding her sound easy, but that wasn't the case. The wind had covered her tracks with snow as soon as she left them, yet something had led him to the ravine where the jeep had rolled over, and with all the snow, there was that one tire clearly exposed. It was really strange.

He shook his head. He'd never have been able to forgive himself if anything had happened to her. She was his best friend's daughter, and no matter how difficult she was, he had to remember that she came from a different world, a world where money talked, and it was evident that Charlene Van Payton had always used her money to get what she wanted. Patience was going to be the key in dealing with her.

A little later Zach checked on Charlene, feeling her skin to be sure she was still warm. He stood over her, noticing how the flames of the fire made her hair glisten gold. She was beautiful, he'd give her that, and he had to admit he felt his heart skip a beat or two when he was stripping her out of her wet clothes. But she wasn't his type, he told himself. He preferred petite, spunky brunettes, not tall, cool blondes.

Zach's train of thought made him remember Monica. Petite, spunky Monica, the girl he thought he'd marry. They'd had so much in common—love of the outdoors, love of horses—but after being together all through college and two years after, Zach had discovered one very important difference. He wanted to settle down and start a family, while Monica wanted to follow her dream of being a singer, and the last thing she wanted in her life *ever* were children.

He'd dated since then, but he'd never gotten serious about anyone, and the last he'd heard, Monica was in Nashville, still trying to get her big break. He wondered if he'd ever get married. He was almost thirty-three, and spending winters alone on this mountain wasn't the best way to meet women. Perhaps Charlene Van Payton was right. Maybe he should sell out and head for the city where women were in abundance.

He shook his head in disgust at his own thoughts. He'd go crazy in some concrete city. This was where he wanted to live and raise his kids.

Zach took his guitar from its case and sat down in front of the fireplace. He began to play one of his favorite classical pieces, letting his mind wander as he remembered the last month of Cody's life. They had talked about his time with Emily Van Payton, and how he had loved her enough to give up everything he cared about, but it hadn't been enough. Cody had admitted that he had been weary of the rodeo circuit and thought the soft life of leisure would suit him, but he had been wrong. He'd found it a waste to have nothing to accomplish each day. Besides that, he hadn't cared for the people the Van Paytons associated with, and particularly hadn't cared for Emily's mother, who browbeat her daughter and everyone else around her. Apparently the only time Emily had ever stood up to her was to marry Cody.

Zach stopped playing and stared into the fire. Cody had said he wanted his daughter to have a chance. Was that why he had deeded half of the ranch to her? He knew Cody had sent Emily a long letter to be delivered after his death. Maybe that had something to do with his daughter being there. Charlene had mentioned that she had been talked into the trip, or, as she put it, into this fiasco. Perhaps her mother, out of some loyalty to Cody, had forced her to come. It was a shame they had picked such an inconvenient time, but then according to Cody, Emily had never been there, so she wouldn't have known the snows came early in Wyoming.

He knelt down and stirred the fire. Hell, why was he trying to figure out what the girl was doing there. She was there and he was going to have to deal with her. If Cody wanted his daughter to know his world, it was up to him to show it to her.

Walking to the side of her bed, he stared down at the sleeping figure in red long johns. The first thing he had to do was find some clothes for her. He smiled. Just wait until she woke up and realized what she was wearing.

TEN

Charlene woke with a start, trying to remember where she was and how she'd gotten there. She felt peculiarly disoriented, remembering the jeep rolling over and being suffocated in a cocoon of snow but unable to remember much after that. Suddenly she glanced down at her attire. "Oh, my God," she moaned, realizing she was wearing a suit of red underwear that was definitely made to fit someone twice her size. How in the world did she get into it?

She closed her eyes and tried to remember what had happened. Slowly one recollection came back of being dragged back and forth in front of the fire by Zach.

The aroma of something delicious cooking made her forget her unattractive outfit. She slowly climbed from the bed, feeling as if she'd been run over by a truck. Walking gingerly on extremely sore feet, she headed for the powder room. Her confrontation with Zach Leighton to get some answers would have to wait a few minutes, she decided.

"Do you mind telling me who put these horrendous things on me?" she asked as she entered the kitchen a few minutes later.

Zach glanced up from his cooking and nearly laughed at the sight of her standing in the doorway holding more than a foot of excess red material out from her stomach. The long johns swallowed her whole, but her beautiful blond hair tumbled around her shoulders in cascades, making her look very desirable. "Well, it wasn't Smoky the Bear, Charley."

"How dare you take advantage of me when I didn't know what I was doing."

Zach laughed. "Lady, you haven't known what you were doing since you left San Francisco. Now sit down and enjoy your last chance to be served breakfast, because after this morning it's your job."

Charlene sniffed the wonderful smells coming from the stove. "We may both starve to death," she said, eyeing the scrambled eggs, ham, and biscuits that Zach set on the table, "but if you're willing to chance it, I'll give it a try."

"Fair enough. Now eat before it gets cold."

Forgetting her dreadful attire, Charlene sat down and ate with a ravenous appetite. "I don't remember much about what happened after the jeep went off the road yesterday. Can you fill in some of the blanks for me?"

"Sure," he said, "but it wasn't yesterday. It was two days ago."

"I've been asleep for two days?" she asked in disbelief.

"Off and on," he answered. "And let me tell you, princess, you're a real pain as a patient."

"I'm sorry, but you certainly can't hold me responsible when I didn't know what I was doing,'' she pointed out.

''I suppose that's plausible,'' he agreed, pouring her a second cup of coffee. In reality, he'd enjoyed taking care of her, but he wasn't going to let her know that.

''You were going to tell me what happened after the jeep went off the road,'' she reminded him.

Zach grinned mischievously. ''You were trapped, I saved you, and now you owe me your life. I believe that means you have to be my slave for the rest of your life.''

Charlene laughed. ''In your dreams, Zach Leighton. Seriously, tell me how you got me back to the lodge.''

''I hooked you to an elk and he dragged you back.''

''Would you be serious,'' she pleaded. ''I would really like to know what happened. I can't remember anything after being trapped in the jeep.''

''I followed you on the snowmobile. Most of your tracks were covered by the drifting snow, but for some reason, I was drawn to the ravine where you went over. The only thing visible on the jeep was one tire. I was scared to death that you were dead, but after digging for about thirty minutes, your hand moved and I knew I still had a partner. I brought you back to the lodge on the snowmobile, warmed you up, forced you to walk for an hour or so, while you complained quite vehemently, I might add, then you slept like the dead, and that's about it.''

Charlene was silent for a long moment. Trying to get off the mountain had been a fool thing to do after all his warnings. ''I'm surprised you're not angry with me, or haven't said you told me so,'' she said, tears welling up in her green eyes.

"I was furious with you when I saw that damned jeep break through the snow, but I calmed down after seeing how close you came to dying."

"Thank you for coming to my rescue. You could have just left me there."

"I know," he grinned. "I thought about it, but you would probably have haunted me until my dying day."

Charlene giggled. "I would have. Since you did save me, we still have to deal with the problem of our partnership."

"It isn't something we have to deal with now," Zach said after he sipped his coffee.

Charlene looked very serious as a memory came back to her. "You know, it was very strange, but I could have sworn I could hear a man's voice telling me to hang on, that I would be fine."

Zach didn't say anything. He'd also been sure something or someone had led him to her jeep, but he'd told himself the cold had made him hallucinate. "I suppose a lot of strange things go through our minds when we are scared or near death."

"Are you referring to one of those near death experiences that predominates daytime talk shows?"

"Yeah, something like that. How about another biscuit?" he said, wanting to change the subject.

Charlene helped herself to a fourth biscuit and lavished it generously with butter and jam.

Zach grinned. "How do you stay so thin with an appetite like that?"

"It's strange," Charlene said, pausing before eating her biscuit. "I've never had a good appetite until now. It must be the fresh air. I'll have to be careful or I'll be fat before I get off this mountain."

"Maybe you'll be like your father," Zach commented between bites. "He ate like a horse, but always stayed trim. He never seemed to tire, at least not until he became ill. Before that he hardly ever sat still. He usually joined the rodeo circuit during the winter because he couldn't stand to be idle here." Charlene didn't comment. "Did your mother ever tell you that you have eyes just like your father's?"

Charlene looked up from her plate. "He had green eyes?"

Zach stared across the table at her. "Yeah, it's pretty eerie. Looking into your eyes is like looking into his."

Charlene sipped her coffee. "Since my mother and grandmother both had blue eyes, I thought my green eyes probably came from his side."

"I have pictures of Cody, if you're interested."

"No . . . No thank you," she said getting up and carrying her dishes to the sink. "They really don't interest me."

"All right," Zach said, following her to the sink with his dishes.

"Oh, God," she moaned. "Where is my masseuse when I need her? Every bone in my body aches." Then she glanced at her nails. "And a good manicure wouldn't hurt."

She looked so ridiculous examining her nails while dressed in red long johns that Zach suddenly began to laugh. Charlene turned around and stared at him. "I'm sorry, but you look like a cross between Mammy Yokum and Daisy Mae."

Charlene had to smile. "I don't know who Mammy

Yokum and Daisy Mae are, but I can imagine from your laugh that that isn't a flattering comparison," she said haughtily. "Besides, you're the one who picked my outfit, Zach Leighton. I did have other nightgowns you could have chosen for me."

Zach laughed. "You mean one of those slinky satin things?"

"That's right."

"You're not going to try to tell me that you would have been warm in one of those."

"No, but I didn't notice you laughing at me when I wore the black one," she pointed out, a mischievous glint in her eyes.

Oh, she was so right, he thought. *The sight of her in that clinging gown had caused him endless hours of tossing and turning, but he wasn't about to tell her that.* "I'm not really laughing at you, princess," he said, looking her up and down. "As a matter of fact, I think you look damned cute."

"Thanks, but your compliment is too late. You already hurt me to the quick," she said, feigning a pout. Suddenly she turned around modeling her long johns as if they were top fashion. "If they could see me now," she laughed as she sang the words to a song. "Do you think this will ever be high fashion for the yacht club? Maybe with a cowboy hat . . ."

Zach smiled, wondering if Charlene Van Payton had ever laughed at herself before. "I don't think so, Charley, but then what do I know?" For some reason, the thought of her back at the yacht club irritated him. "It's time for me to check on the cabins. When I come back we'll play some cards, if you like."

"Oh, wonderful. I haven't played bridge since college, but how will we play with just two people?"

"I wasn't talking about bridge, Lady Van Payton. I was talking about poker."

"Bridge is the only game I know."

"Then I'll teach you to play poker."

"Isn't poker gambling?" she asked innocently. "I believe I remember my grandmother saying poker wasn't a game a lady played."

"Well, ma'am, that all depends on how you play it. There's regular poker, and then there's strip poker, and since you don't know how to play either, I think you should learn both," he said with a twinkle in his blue eyes. "See you in a little while."

Zach found himself hurrying through the usual thorough check he made on the cabins, whistling as he quickly checked the pipes. Suddenly he remembered the clothes for Charlene. He headed for the cabin the wranglers had used, hoping one of the girls had left some items behind as they often did. Charley was taller than either of the two girls who worked for the ranch, but he hoped to come up with something she wouldn't feel ridiculous wearing.

Two shirts, some faded jeans, and a pair of well-worn boots later, Zach headed back toward the lodge. He found Charlene curled up on the couch in front of the fire sound asleep.

He touched a strand of her hair, letting it slip through his fingers. "Sleeping Beauty," he whispered with a sigh.

"Did you say something?" Charlene asked as she stretched like a cat.

"No, nothing. I didn't mean to wake you."

"I don't seem to have any energy," she said as she sat up, stretching again.

"That's understandable. You're still suffering the aftereffects of nearly being killed." He laid the clothes on the end of the couch. "I found a few things that might fit you, and you're welcome to anything I have."

"Thank you. You didn't by any chance find any cigarettes?"

"Sorry," he said as he put a log on the fire. "No cigarettes."

Charlene sighed. "Maybe I could have my mother drop a care package from a plane."

Zach stared at her in disbelief. "Tell me you're kidding."

"I need a cigarette, Zach," she said, as if that would make him understand such a rash statement.

"And you'd have someone fly from California to drop you a pack of cigarettes? My God, woman, I can't believe anyone could be so selfish or spoiled. Why don't you stop thinking about yourself for a change and think about the poor pilot who would have to do your bidding, not to mention the cost to your company."

"I don't need this abuse, Zach Leighton!" she shouted, rubbing her temples. "I've listened to all your lectures on morals and principles that I care to."

"You make it sound as if principles are something to be ashamed of," he yelled back at her.

"I didn't say that, and don't yell at me, Zach Leighton. It's your fault I'm here."

"My fault? How the hell is it my fault?" he asked in disbelief.

"You . . . you could have sold me the ranch the day I arrived, and then I wouldn't have had to stay," she blurted out irrationally.

Zach's eyes glinted dangerously, and for a brief moment he considered shaking her until she got some sense in her head, but instead he grabbed his jacket and stormed out of the lodge.

Charlene sat there staring at the fire, tears running down her face. How dare the man talk to her like a child. Didn't he realize how hard it was to go cold turkey without a cigarette? He didn't have to be so unreasonable and self-righteous about everything. If he wasn't so insensitive he could see she was in pain.

"Damn," she hissed, slamming her fist on the arm of the sofa. How could she be expected to get along with the man? He was hardheaded and thoughtless. He should have known she wouldn't really have cigarettes flown in. She was just feeling desperate and trapped.

She sat there for a long moment going over their conversation. *Well, maybe he wasn't thoughtless. He had found her some clothes, and told her she could wear any of his things.*

Charlene sighed. Maybe if she tried to fix dinner it would take her mind off of not having a cigarette, and at the same time pacify her angry partner. "Humph," she snorted. Once she bought his part of the ranch she wouldn't have to deal with Mr. Zachariah Leighton. *But was that what she really wanted*? a little voice asked.

ELEVEN

Zach walked until he had cooled off. He really didn't know why he had blown up at Charlene the way he had. He knew the girl had been spoiled rotten all her life. Why should it have surprised him that she wanted to have cigarettes flown in?

Maybe because you keep hoping she'll change, he thought, taking a deep breath of air. "Why the hell should I care?" he said aloud. "She means nothing to me."

But then common sense kicked in, and he stopped to think about what made her tick. For twenty-one years everyone had been at her beck and call. She had been taught that her money could get her anything she wanted. How could he expect her to change in a few days? He kicked a pile of snow, furious with himself. He had said he was going to be patient with her for Cody's sake, and look how he reacted.

A frown creased his handsome brow. God, what was it about this girl that had him walking aimlessly around in zero-degree weather talking to himself? He picked up a handful of snow and made a snowball, then threw it hard against the side of the stables. He remembered how hard it was to stop smoking. The girl was probably going through hell, on top of still being in shock from nearly being killed. How could he be such an insensitive bastard? If he didn't start showing a little patience with her he was going to be taking a lot of walks in freezing weather. They were in too close proximity not to try to get along, he told himself as he headed back to the lodge. Cody had a reason for making them partners, though he sure as hell couldn't imagine what it was, so he had to make the best of it.

When he opened the door, the smell of something burning filled the lodge. "Charlene! Are you all right?" he shouted, panic in his voice.

"I'm in the kitchen and could use your help."

Zach rushed into the kitchen, finding the room filled with smoke, but no flames. "Good Lord, I thought the place was on fire. What happened?"

"I was fixing pork chops and boiled potatoes, just like the cookbook instructed, but I'm afraid I got a little overwhelmed," she said, fighting back tears. "The pork chops burned to a crisp while I was trying to peel potatoes."

Zach smiled, pleased that she had tried to cook dinner for them. "Are the potatoes all right?"

Charlene looked surprised by his question. "Yes, they're fine."

"Then no problem. We'll whip up an omelet and fry the potatoes with some onions. It's one of my favorite meals."

Charlene stared at him for a long moment, then began to cry. "Just stop," she said on a sob.

Zach was taken completely aback. "For God's sake, Charlene, what's wrong? What did I say?"

"I'm a failure at everything," she sobbed, "and you're still being nice to me. Did you forget that thirty minutes ago I ran you out of your own home with my ravings? Go ahead, yell at me. Tell me I can't do anything right."

Zach pulled her into his arms and stroked her hair. "You're not a failure, Charley. Regardless of what we perceive as personal shortcomings or failings, all of us have something we do that makes our lives worthwhile. You're just having a hard time now because you're suffering nicotine withdrawal symptoms. That's all it is. I remember when I was quitting, none of my friends wanted to be around me. I was miserable for about five days, then I felt fine. As a matter of fact, I've felt ten times better since I kicked the habit."

"Really?" Charlene asked, staring into his eyes.

"Really. Now sit down here, and let me find you something to drink. Who knows, maybe I'll be able to come up with some wine. Wine and eggs are a strange combination, but there are times you need to live dangerously."

"I don't need anything," she said with a sniff.

"Well, I do."

"I'm sorry." She began to cry again. "Now I've driven you to drink."

Zach laughed. "Don't be ridiculous, Charley. Ah, just as I thought, Cody did have a couple of bottles of wine stashed in the cupboard." After rummaging through the drawer for a corkscrew, he opened the bottle and poured them both a glass. "This will make you feel better."

Charlene took a sip. "Thank you. I haven't been successful fixing a meal yet," she said in a warbly voice. "Maybe I can set the table without ruining something."

"Stop being so hard on yourself, Charley," he said with a tender smile. "You're doing just fine. How about looking in the freezer and see if you can find me a bag of green peppers?" he suggested. "You do like onions and peppers, don't you?"

"Yes, anything is fine," she said, handing him the bag. "I tried to call my mother while you were out."

"Is she going to send you some cigarettes?" Zach asked as he chopped onions.

"I wasn't serious about that, Zach," she explained. "I was just feeling desperate."

"I know," he said gently. "I should have realized that. Well, what did your mother have to say?"

"She wasn't there," Charlene said with a long sigh, as she took extra care to fold their napkins. "She was on a trip to Seattle."

Zach glanced at her, noticing the tears in her eyes again. "I'm sorry, Charley."

"It doesn't matter," she sighed with a shrug of the shoulders. "She's never been there when I needed someone to talk to. It isn't her fault, really. I think she works twenty-four hours a day so she won't think about how unhappy or lonely she is. When I used to complain to my grandmother about being lonely and needing friends, she'd have my nanny buy me an expensive gift, as if that would take care of everything."

Her admission tugged at Zach's heart, and he silently cursed himself again for having lost his temper with her earlier. "You can talk to me anytime you want. I've always been a good listener."

Charlene smiled sadly at him. "Thanks, but I think you're what's known as a captive audience."

"I want to get to know you, Charley," he said with sincerity. "Cody must have had a reason for making you and me partners, so why don't we make the best of it?"

"You don't have to pretend to want to be my friend," she said, studying the contents of her glass. "I know you think I'm just a spoiled, pampered rich girl who has had everything all her life, but let me tell you, just because you have material things doesn't necessarily mean you're happy."

"Maybe you've been going about finding happiness the wrong way," he suggested.

"Maybe I have," she said with a shrug of her shoulders. "If you had all the money in the world, what would you do to be happy?"

Zach thought for a long moment. "If I had money, I'd want to help others less fortunate than myself, and I'd become involved in important environmental issues, funding programs to explore every possible way to clean up our planet. I'd work to get my wealthy friends involved, too. Most wealthy people forget that they can help immensely with time and funds. They're too involved in their own lives to even think about the possibility of the world being ruined for their children or grandchildren.

"I never thought much about it," she admitted as he set their food on the table.

"That's the problem. Most people don't think

about it. Try your omelet and see if it's to your liking."

"I'm sure it will be," she said. "Ummm, delicious. You keep trying to make me your cook, but you end up doing it all."

"You can try again tomorrow morning," he said, taking a bite. "This is what I always rely on when I don't feel like cooking anything else."

"Do you get tired of cooking and eating alone?"

"I have to admit it's always nicer to share a meal with someone. I had four brothers and two sisters, and mealtime was always an experience," he said with a laugh. "Fortunately my family were farmers, so we always had enough to eat, even if we didn't have much else."

"Does your family live around here?" she asked.

"No. My parents died in an automobile accident several years ago, and the rest of my family are spread all over the country."

"I'm sorry about your parents," she said softly. "I know it's terrible to be alone. I had my grandmother and mother, but I always ate alone or with a nanny until I was old enough to go out and eat with people at the club. My mother has always traveled a lot, or when she wasn't traveling she was working, and my grandmother took all her meals in her room."

"It's a shame they didn't let you spend summers with Cody when he asked. You would have loved it here."

"My father wanted me to spend summers with him?" she asked in disbelief. "What possible reason could my mother have had for not letting me come? She never was able to spend much time with me."

"Cody didn't think your mother was aware that he was trying to arrange to spend time with you. He believed your grandmother and her lawyers were the ones always putting roadblocks in his way. Every time he tried to contact your mother he was told that she was out of the country. Your grandmother only let him see you twice, but on those visits she made sure you were so unhappy that Cody felt guilty and finally gave up trying to visit you."

"I don't remember ever seeing him," she said thoughtfully. "I must have been very young."

"I believe he told me you were two the last time he saw you," Zach said, putting his empty plate to the side.

"I don't understand why no one ever told me that he'd tried to see me. I wish I had known."

"I know," Zach said, placing his hand over hers. "I've been trying to tell you that Cody wasn't the villain you thought he was. He loved you, and it ate at him not being able to see or know you."

Charlene was silent for a long moment. "My mother and I have some serious talking to do when I get back to San Francisco."

"Good idea," Zach said. "Now how about some black walnut ice cream for dessert?"

"Sounds wonderful," she said, feeling much better. "I noticed you have a good supply of meat and vegetables in the freezer. Did you stock it yourself?"

"No, I can't take credit for it. We have a wonderful cook who took care of that. We grow a lot of our own vegetables, and even raise hormone-free beef on the ranch. Paul, our cook, makes sure I have a big variety of things to eat so I don't get bored. When I'm tired of meat or eggs, I can always fish. The trout around here are incredible tasting. We'll have to go fishing soon. You'll love it."

Charlene smiled. "I can't imagine loving it, but I'll reserve my opinion until I try it."

Zach laughed. "Fair enough."

"You mentioned that you worked to save the environment. Tell me more about that. What is it you're trying to accomplish?"

As Zach dished out ice cream, he began to talk. "I've spent years trying to make people see what they're doing, but they don't want to listen. We're ruining the rivers and oceans with pollution, cutting down our forests, destroying the rain forest at an incredible rate, filling our land with trash that will never disintegrate, and yet very few people even blink an eye at what is happening."

"I can see why you went to Washington," she commented as she took a bite of ice cream. "You are very passionate about what you believe."

"Unfortunately, that's also why I left Washington. No one wanted to listen, or even gave a damn. I decided to come back here and see that my own piece of the world was well taken care of. We have environmental problems in Wyoming, too, but we're trying to deal with them. One person can make a difference, Charlene. One person at a time realizing that they must do something, even if it's infinitesimal, we all have to do something before it's too late."

Charlene could see the passion in his eyes when he spoke about the environment, and she envied him having something that meant so much to him.

"I want to know more, Zach. Maybe when I get back to San Francisco I can help in some way."

"Are you serious?"

"Yes," she answered, tears welling in her eyes. "When I nearly died, I began to think how I had been wasting my life. I spent most of my time either trying to prove myself to my mother or feeling sorry for myself, at which time I'd go on a shopping spree. I want to change that, Zach. I'm not sure how, but I can't go on the way I have been. Do you know, I have never had a real friend," she admitted, "but I realized that I've never given my friendship to anyone. I'm going to make it a point to change that when I go back home."

Zach's heart went out to her. "I'd like to be your friend," he offered. "I think that may be why Cody made us partners in this ranch. Maybe he thought we could help each other."

Charlene laughed through her tears. "How could I possibly help you, Zach? You seem perfectly content with your life."

Zach thought about telling her how wrong she was, but he wasn't ready to open up to her yet. "Everyone needs friends, Charlene. Maybe Cody felt I was spending too much time alone."

Charlene held her wineglass up to his. "Then here's to friendships."

Zach touched his glass to hers. "And to Cody Jones."

Charlene stared into Zach's eyes, then finally smiled. "To Cody Jones."

[illegible]

[illegible] never thought to explore any farther than the space

TWELVE

Zach glanced at Charlene, who seemed absorbed in a book. She had her feet curled up under her and kept twisting a piece of hair as she read, reminding him of one of his sisters when she was a teenager.

For the past week they each had made a concerted effort to get along, but it hadn't always been easy. There were times when he had to bite his tongue to keep from losing his patience with her, particularly when he had asked her to make her bed and she had informed him she had never made a bed. Another time he had suggested she put a load of wash in while he chopped wood, and she had looked at him like he was asking her to go to the moon. She had a way of pushing him to the limits with her naiveté, and sometimes he wondered if she'd been raised in a secluded monastery. She seemed completely oblivious to the world around her, and apparently had never thought to explore any farther than the space between the Van Payton mansion and the Van Payton headquarters.

She had told him she enjoyed sailing and playing golf, but somehow he doubted if she'd really ever done either. He had the feeling she had heard people at her club talking about these sports, and she had assumed they were the things affluent people did. From conversations they had had, it didn't seem to him like she knew anything about the sea, or even the San Francisco Bay. She had been horrified when he told her how dolphins and whales were needlessly killed by Japanese fishermen. She claimed she had never heard such a thing.

He had to admit, he was pleased that she was like a sponge, absorbing everything he told her about his work for the environment, and about the ranch and her father. She was actually excited about getting involved in environmental issues when she returned to San Francisco.

It was strange how things worked out. He had been sure he could never enjoy her company because she was so spoiled and pampered, yet he actually found her to be a very pleasant companion. After she'd discovered that he wasn't the country bumpkin he had pretended to be, he'd also had to admit to her that he'd lied about some of his likes and dislikes, including the fact that he enjoyed classical music. They had spent several evenings playing the classical discs he had, and discussing their favorite composers. He had also introduced her to country music, and even some new age music, and she had readily accepted it.

"Zach, let's do something," she said, breaking into his thoughts. "I'm tired of reading."

"What do you want to do?"

"You promised to take me for a ride on the snowmobile," she reminded him. "How about now?"

"It's mighty cold out," he warned.

"I know, but you've insisted I stay in all this week and I'm getting cabin fever. It will be fun to come back here and curl up in front of the fire afterward."

"That sounds good, but we won't stay out more than thirty minutes. I don't want to take any chances on you getting too cold. Your hands and feet are still going to be sensitive to the cold."

"I promise as soon as I start to get cold I'll tell you. Stop being such a mother hen," she scolded with a smile. "When we come back, why don't we have dinner in front of the fire, and maybe play some cards? If I keep practicing I just might beat you yet," she warned with a grin.

"No chance, lady," he said, holding out his hand to help her off the sofa. "I'll go get the snowmobile while you put on another layer of clothes, and be sure to get another pair of socks out of my drawer. Two pairs will protect those delicate toes."

Charlene laughed. "Get out of here, cowboy. I'll meet you out front in a few minutes. After I add those clothes I want to check on dinner before we go."

When Charlene was bundled up, and dinner was in the oven, she headed out front. Discovering that Zach wasn't there yet, she headed down the hill toward the stables. As she walked, she kept thinking she saw something moving out of the side of her vision. She stopped and the movement stopped. Moving closer, she was surprised to discover a gaunt-looking, large gray dog. "Oh, you poor thing. You look starved." The dog continued to eye her suspiciously. "Come on," she coaxed. "Come back to the lodge with me and I'll find you some food. Come on now," she urged, snapping her fingers as she walked backward, trying to get the dog to follow her. "You can trust me. I won't hurt you. We'll just get you some food and you can be on your way if you still want to, or you can stay."

Zach hadn't been able to get the snowmobile to start and was heading back to the lodge to get a spark plug when he saw Charlene. He couldn't believe his eyes. She was coaxing a wolf to follow her to the lodge.

"I've never had a pet," she was telling the wolf. "If you want to hang around I'm sure we can find enough leftovers to put some weight on those bones."

"Charlene, don't move."

"Oh, Zach, I'm glad you're here," she said, missing the warning tone of his voice. "This poor dog looks like he's starving. I'm trying to get it to come back to the lodge so I can feed it. Will you help me?"

Zach slowly moved to stand beside her. "You can't feed it," he said softly.

Charlene stared at him in disbelief. "How can you be so cruel? We have some leftovers the dog could have. It's not going to take food out of your mouth."

"Charlene," he said, trying to be patient, "this is not a dog. It's a wolf, the animal that's been keeping you awake at night."

Charlene glanced back at the wary animal, who

seemed to be listening to them. "That's a . . . a wolf?"

"Sure is, and the rest of the pack are probably nearby. They stay pretty close together."

"Well, the poor thing still looks hungry," she persisted. "Why don't I just get our leftovers and feed him and his pack?"

"That's very compassionate of you, but it's the worst thing you could do. They have to remain wild and not depend on people to feed them, otherwise they'd starve to death."

"But why would feeding him cause him to starve to death?"

"He'd become dependent on humans to feed him, and most humans only feed on an impulse. When the cuteness wears off, the animal is left on his own again. By that time his digestive system has been fouled up by toxins in our foods, and he has come to prefer the ease of letting humans take care of his needs. It happens all the time in our parks and woodlands."

"I never thought of that," she mused.

"Most people don't."

"Are they always that thin?"

"Yes, but believe me, he's not starving. Wolves cover a lot of ground in a day and stay trim."

Charlene continued to stare at the animal. "He's really very beautiful. His eyes are so penetrating and expressive. When he looks at me it seems he can see into my soul."

"I told you there was a mystical quality to them. We came very close to making them extinct in this area. About fifty years ago our government decided all wolves in Yellowstone Park and surrounding areas should be exterminated."

"Exterminated?" she exclaimed. "My God, why?"

"They claimed they were trying to improve nature, but it was a grave ecological mistake. Now they're trying desperately to return the wolf to its native home, and at the same time restore the park's natural balance."

"That's just incredible," she said, staring at the wolf. "How could anyone want to kill them?"

"It's something I've never understood," he answered, smiling at her. *You've come a long way, Charlene Van Payton*, he thought, remembering their first conversation about her fur coat.

"He looks so much like a large dog."

"Yes, most do. Now when you hear them at night, maybe you won't be afraid."

Without thinking, Charlene took Zach's hand. "I'm getting better about that," she said proudly. "You make me feel very safe and secure."

"Do I?" he asked, a lump in his throat, thinking that he'd miss holding her at night when she was no longer afraid. *My God, where did that come from?* he wondered. *What a fool you are*, a little voice laughed at him. *You desire the girl. Why do you think all those cold showers have been necessary?*

"Zach, did you hear me?" Charlene asked.

"I'm sorry. What did you say?"

"I said I think I'll be able to sleep without the light on soon."

He laughed, trying to gather his thoughts about him. "You've come a long way, baby," he teased.

"I have, haven't I?" she said with a grin on her lovely face. "I'm sure Cody didn't know about my fears, but if it hadn't been for him insisting I come here, I wouldn't be making progress."

"I told you there was a method to his madness when he threw the two of us together. Look . . ." Zach directed her attention to where the wolf had been standing.

"It's gone," she exclaimed in disbelief. "I didn't even hear it move."

"Maybe it disappeared in thin air," he whispered mysteriously.

"Oh, stop," she laughed, pushing against him. "You're trying to spook me."

Zach pulled her against him. "Would I do something like that, Charley?" he asked softly.

Charlene stared into his blue eyes, suddenly feeling the change that was taking place in their relationship. She was drawn to him, but she was so unfamiliar with the feeling she couldn't understand it. Her heart was doing flips and her knees suddenly felt like they'd turned to water. She drew a deep breath, trying to steady her nerves. "What happened to that snowmobile?" she asked in a shaky voice.

"It wouldn't start," he answered, releasing her. "I was on my way back to get a new spark plug from the lodge when I saw you trying to befriend that wolf."

Charlene smiled. "I have a lot to learn, don't I?"

"You might say that," he said, tweaking her nose playfully. "Let's forget that ride for today and just take a walk. I'll fix the snowmobile in the morning."

"All right," she readily agreed. "I already put the ham in the oven, so we shouldn't stay out too much longer."

"Did you turn the oven on?" he teased.

"Of course," she answered indignantly. Suddenly a worried expression came over her pretty face. "At least I think so. Maybe I should go back and check."

"Forget it," he laughed, pulling her along. "I'm getting used to eggs."

"Tonight is going to be different," she promised. "I've been studying the cookbook, and I'm prepared to make sweet potatoes and green beans to go with the ham."

"Good for you," Zach praised her. "When you leave here you'll be a gourmet cook."

"I don't know about that, but I have to admit I've enjoyed the challenge. Tomorrow I'm going to try to bake a cake," she said with enthusiasm. "I'm getting over the worst of the nicotine withdrawal, but now I find I'm craving sweets."

"That will pass, too," he assured her, tightening his hold on her hand. "I'm really proud of the way you've kicked the habit. It took a lot of guts."

Charlene laughed. "If you recall, Mr. Leighton, I didn't have a choice. There wasn't a cigarette within ten miles."

"I know," he said, giving her a teasing grin. "I hope you'll stick with it when you go back to San Francisco."

"I plan to," she said, smiling up at him. "I told you things were going to change."

Zach studied her lovely face, thinking things had already changed. There suddenly seemed to be a sexual awareness between them, at least on his part, and he thought she felt the same thing, or was that just wishful thinking? he wondered.

"Zach, what is that?" she whispered breathlessly, directing his attention behind him.

Zach glanced up the hill. "It's an elk," he said softly. "Thousands of them come through here each winter heading for the Elk refuge in Jackson."

"He's so majestic-looking," she exclaimed. "I can't believe in less than thirty minutes we've seen a wolf and an elk."

He laughed softly. "It's a little different from San Francisco's wildlife, eh? Well, Lady Van Payton, for your information, Wyoming is known for its wildlife. At last count there were reported to be three hundred and forty species of birds, one hundred species of mammals, and seventy-eight species of fish."

"You sound like a tour guide for Wyoming."

"I guess I do. It's because I love it here. I'm from South Dakota, which is a fine state, but from the first time I came to this area I felt its hold on me. The Tetons are like no mountains I'd ever seen. Sometime when I look at them I feel as if I've been here in another time, another life." He laughed. "That sounds crazy, doesn't it?"

"I don't think so. I think it's nice to like where you live. I've never thought much about it," she admitted.

"I can't think of any place I'd rather live and raise a family."

"Oh," Charlene said, glancing at him sideways. "Have you . . ." She cleared her throat. "Do you have someone . . . someone special . . . I mean, someone you plan to marry?"

"I came close once," he admitted, "but it didn't work out."

Charlene stifled a relieved giggle. "Did the lucky young lady realize in time what a country bumpkin you were?"

He grinned at her lazily, wondering if she'd ever had the opportunity to tease before. "Something like that," he answered, "but I'm only thirty-three, so I figure I still have time to find the right woman and have a bunch of kids."

"I pity the poor woman who marries you," Charlene said, shaking her head. "Sounds like you're looking for a baby machine."

Zach laughed. "That's not true. I'm just like any other man. I want a beautiful, intelligent, sensitive woman who will cook, clean, chop wood, raise the kids, and keep me happy."

"Oh, my word, it's worse than I thought."

"How about you, Charley? Have you ever thought about marrying and having kids?"

Charlene smiled faintly, her eyes reflecting a sudden sadness. "No, not really. I've been involved in learning my family's business, and haven't given much thought to anything else. Besides, my family hasn't had very good luck with relationships."

"That doesn't mean you won't," Zach commented. "In the past week I've learned that there is more to you than just a successful, beautiful woman. I'm sure some man will come along and realize the same thing, and sweep you off your feet."

Zach's eyes were guilelessly sincere as he spoke, making Charlene feel warm and cared for. "Do you really think so?" she asked innocently.

"I'm sure of it," he said with a teasing smile. "And don't forget, by the time you leave here you'll be an excellent cook, able to make a bed, and maybe even chop some wood."

"Oh, you," she laughed. "I suppose next you're going to tell me I can also practice making you happy.'' As soon as she said it, she realized the implication of her words. ''I mean, you'd want me to . . . to scrub floors . . . or something.''

Zach smiled as she tried to disentangle herself from her statement. ''You can practice making me happy anytime you want, Charley,'' he said with a laugh. ''Come on, I'm freezing.'' He grabbed her by the hand. ''I'm looking forward to sitting in front of that fire. I think we should open another bottle of wine this evening. Don't you?''

Charlene didn't even hear his question. Her mind was filled with pictures of her sitting in front of the fire with Zach, practicing her feminine wiles on him.

THIRTEEN

When dinner was over they both sat on the sofa in front of the fire, listening to a classical compact disc.

Charlene watched Zach drink his wine, thinking how sensuous his mouth was. What would his lips feel like on hers? Would he run his tongue over her lips lightly, or would he be more aggressive? When Zach glanced at her and smiled, Charlene quickly looked away, chastising herself for letting her imagination run wild. It was disconcerting enough to be isolated with the man, without starting to have sexual fantasies about him.

"Dinner was excellent tonight, Charley."

"Thank you," she said without looking at him.

"Is everything all right?" he asked softly, lifting her chin and forcing her to look at him.

The touch made her senses reel. My God, what was wrong with her? she wondered frantically. She had only had sex once in her life, and hadn't been impressed with the act. Why now did this man's look make all her hormones rage? "I'm fine," she said, trying to keep her voice normal. He moved his hand to the back of her neck, gently massaging the warm skin beneath her hair. "Zach . . ." she blurted out, jumping to her feet. "I . . . I think I'd like to see those photographs you mentioned the other day."

Zach smiled, a look that told her he understood. He stood up and took a large album down from the bookshelf and handed it to her. "Most of them were taken during Cody's rodeo days, but a few of them are later shots with some of our guests," he explained.

Charlene silently looked through the photographs. Zach made no comment, waiting for her to say something. He knew it must be hard for her, yet he felt looking through the album was a good start to her healing process. Sooner or later she had to come to grips with the situation that had left her fatherless. If she could only forgive Cody and understand what he had gone through. It wasn't that he didn't love his daughter. He did, but unfortunately he had let her powerful family convince him that she was better off without him, a mistake they both apparently paid for dearly.

"He was a very handsome man." Charlene finally spoke in a choked voice.

"Yes, he was," Zach agreed. "You look a lot like him."

"Where was this picture of the two of you taken?" she asked, holding up one of the photographs.

Zach glanced at it. "That was taken in Oklahoma at one of the rodeos. Cody had just beaten me out of cowboy of the year by setting a world record in bull riding."

Charlene looked up at him, her green eyes wide with surprise. "You mean you did this rodeo thing, too?"

"Sure did. All through high school and college. That's how I met Cody."

"What is bull riding?" she asked, going back to the picture.

Zach laughed. "Well, let me tell you, sweetheart," he said in his best John Wayne imitation, "it's when a cowboy sits on top of a ton of twisting, pounding muscle, bone, and guts, and tries to hold on for a full eight seconds, and then attempts to get out of the arena before the bull's vicious horns can disembowel him."

"Oh, that sounds like fun," Charlene said sarcastically. "Why would anyone do such a thing?"

"Ah," he said, a mischievous grin on his handsome face. "You would be amazed how women seek out the rodeo cowboys. There were times I had to beat them off with a stick."

Charlene laughed. "In your dreams maybe. Now tell me really why you'd do such a thing." she persisted.

"I suppose it was the danger and excitement," he mused. "Every time I'd crawl over into the chute and lower myself onto the wide back of that snorting, angry animal, I'd feel sick to my stomach and my hair would stand on end, yet at the same time it was the most exciting feeling I'd ever experienced. And when the ride was over and you made it safely out of the arena, you felt like you'd just tempted fate and won."

Charlene shook her head. "I think you were both crazy."

"I suppose you're right," he agreed, "and I have the scars to prove how crazy it was, but I wouldn't trade the experience for all the world."

"You have scars?" she asked, concern on her face. "Are you in pain?"

"Sometimes, but it's not too bad. My left knee gives me trouble now and then, but I was luckier than a lot of others. I've often wondered if one of Cody's injuries could have led to his tumor. He was dumped on his head more than once."

Charlene didn't say anything, but he could tell she was thinking about her father. "Who is this woman with Cody?" she asked, holding up another photo.

"That's Jacqueline Hastings, a Los Angeles lawyer who was here a few years ago. She fell really hard for Cody and pursued him relentlessly, but he wasn't interested in anything permanent."

"I wonder why?" she mused. "She's beautiful."

"To be honest with you, I don't think Cody ever got over your mother, but he wouldn't admit that. It was strange, though, even after all he went through, when he talked about her, his face would actually glow, and he never had an unkind word about her."

Charlene was silent for a long moment. "My mother has never been one to show her feelings, but after she learned that Cody had died, she was extremely upset. I'm afraid I wasn't very understanding about it," she admitted sadly. "As a matter of fact, I wouldn't even listen to her. I told her I didn't want to hear about him because he had never been there for me."

Zach moved closer to her. "I think that's natural. You didn't know that your father had tried to see you."

Charlene looked up from the photograph album to stare into his blue eyes. "Why have you been so nice to me the last couple of days, Zach? Are you trying to soften me up so I'll sell you my part of the ranch?"

Zach laughed. "I probably couldn't afford to pay what you'd ask. No, I think we're going to have to just settle for being partners, Charley, but remember, this isn't a surrender, just a truce."

Charlene smiled. "Do you really think we could ever work together? I want to turn this place into a resort, and I know you'd never agree to that."

He surprised himself with his next statement. "No, I couldn't agree to that because I know what people who come to this area are expecting, Charley, but I wouldn't be opposed to some changes. I think your suggestion of a hot tub would be a nice addition, and the cabins could do with some remodeling. Maybe a woman's touch in decorating would be nice, but keep in mind that people expect a ranch to be rustic in decor."

"And the indoor pool?"

"You're pushing your luck, Lady Van Payton," he said with a smile. "An indoor pool is not on my list of priorities at the moment. I'd rather remodel the bathroom and kitchen in the lodge, and I've been thinking about building a large fire pit in the center of the front deck so people could sit out there on cool evenings and enjoy the view of the Tetons."

"I think that would be a nice addition," Charlene agreed, having found the view breathtaking from the front deck.

"There is one other point," Zach commented. "The last thing Cody did was to buy several Arabian horses to add to our stable. The Arabians' endurance and intelligence fit in perfectly with the terrain around here. Cody had hoped in a few years to have nothing but Arabians, and I'd like to continue that dream for him. Cody had his eye on a beautiful black stallion at the ranch where the horses stay for the winter. I'd particularly like to purchase him so we can improve our stock."

"I don't see any problems with your changes," she said, pleased that they had been able to discuss the ranch without arguing. "You see, we can compromise on what we each want."

Zach lifted a strand of her gold hair and rubbed it between his fingers. "Compromise is good," he said with a smile, "but the Roman baths and pink-and-white cottages are out."

"How about the tennis courts and putting greens?" she asked with a teasing grin.

He shrugged. "We'll have to talk about that down the road, Charley. Maybe we can work something out."

"Down the road?" she asked innocently. "Why do we have to be down the road to talk about it?"

Zach laughed. "It means in the future, princess. The lodge does very well financially during the tourist season, but that's only from May to September. I've saved some money, and Cody left quite a bit to keep the lodge financially secure, but these big remodeling jobs may have to be done over a period of time."

"Money isn't a problem now, Zach. You have a wealthy partner who is willing to make improvements."

A worried look came over Zach's face. "I know you're wealthy, Charley, but we'll still have to work something out where you're not paying for everything. We're partners, and as long as I can pay for half of what we're doing, I'll go along with the improvements."

Charlene suddenly laughed, yet tears were in her eyes. "I can't believe that we're sitting here discussing what we're going to do as partners. If you had told me a few days ago that this would happen, I'd never have believed you."

"Neither would I," Zach admitted, thinking that sometimes a woman could get underneath a man's skin without him even being aware of it.

"I'll have to come back during the season to see this place when it isn't buried in snow," Charlene said.

For some reason he couldn't explain even to himself the thought of her leaving made him feel as if the wind had been knocked out of him. Of course she would leave when the weather allowed. She was his partner, but she'd be living and working in San Francisco. It was probably better that way, he told himself. This temporary truce that they had was only because they were isolated and couldn't do anything about it. She'd return to being the same rich, pampered heiress she'd been when she arrived in Wyoming. Then why did he hate the thought of her leaving?

"Is there something wrong, Zach?" Charlene asked. "Are you having second thoughts?"

"No second thoughts," he assured her. "Your father made this decision for us, so we'll have to make the best of it. If there is any concern on my part, it's wondering how it will work out with you in San Francisco and me here."

Would you want me here? she wondered silently. The truth was, she had begun to enjoy her time there. She actually felt like a bird released from its cage. But she wasn't ready to admit that to Zach. He was probably still anxious to be rid of her, even though he had been extremely nice to her the past few days.

"So what do you think, Charley?"

She jumped at his words. "Think? Think about what?"

Zach laughed. "About you being in San Francisco and my being here. Do you think it will work?"

"Oh, yes, I'm sure it will work out fine. If you think it would help, maybe I could come for a few weeks." *Or months,* she thought. "You'll have to teach me to ride."

"It will be my pleasure," he said in a warm, sexy voice, while moving his thumb gently along her jawline. He smiled when his double entendre went right over her head.

She was staring at him silently, her sea-green eyes oddly speculative. "What are you thinking, Zach?" she asked softly.

"Probably what every man who sees you ends up thinking," he said, a teasing grin touching his mouth.

She drew a deep breath and turned away. "And what is that, that I'm an overbearing, selfish, pampered rich girl? That's what most men think when they meet me."

Zach smiled. "I suppose that was my first impression, too, but that wasn't what I was thinking just now. I was thinking what a beautiful woman you are, and that I'd like to kiss you."

"Zach," she sighed. "I have to admit, I've come

to feel very close to you, and I'll admit when you touch me it's very exciting, but I don't think we should let this happen."

"What is it you think is going to happen?" he asked, his voice warm and intimate, while he caressed her neck.

"If you keep touching me like that, we both know what I think is going to happen."

Zach grinned at her lazily. "Are you a virgin, Charley?"

"I'm twenty-one years old," she said indignantly.

"That doesn't answer my question, Charley."

"No, I'm not a virgin," she admitted softly. "I had sex with a young man last year after we attended a dance."

"Just that one time?"

"Yes," she answered with a sigh, partially annoyed that he was questioning her about such a personal matter, yet also excited by the conversation. "I haven't dated very much."

"Didn't you date the boys you went to school with?"

"Through the first twelve years of school I had tutors that came to our house, and then I attended an all girls college."

That explains a lot, Zach thought. No wonder she was so naive. "Didn't you ever feel that you were missing a lot not going to school with other kids your age?"

"Of course I did, but there wasn't anything I could do about it. It was what my grandmother wanted. I suppose she was only trying to protect me, but that fact didn't help when I was so lonely I could have died. Then when I was able to get out and make my own friends, I suppose I got a little wild. It was only a little bit of freedom, but I felt like I had been let out of prison. I tried smoking, drinking, anything that had been denied me."

"I'm surprised you didn't rebel by having sex with every young man you met," Zach commented.

Charlene laughed bitterly. "I live in an area where AIDS runs rampant, and that fact makes you think twice before you go to bed with just anyone."

"Very smart thinking. Did the young man use protection?" he asked bluntly.

"Zach, for God's sake, what is this, the Inquisition?" she asked defensively. "Yes, he used protection. Now, while we're being so honest with each other, why don't you tell me about your sex life?"

"I don't go in for one-night stands, but I have had a few relationships where we were sexually active."

"Did you use protection?" she asked, trying to be as clinical as he was.

"Yes, for the past ten years I have."

"Very smart thinking," she said, using his words. Her nerves felt as if they were exposed. She'd never felt such sexual awareness before. Zach's hand lightly touching her shoulder felt as if it were burning her skin. "So where do we go from here?" she asked tremulously.

"We go very slowly," he said, surprising her. "As I said, I don't like one-night stands. If we start a relationship, it's going to mean something."

Charlene swallowed. "Are you sure this isn't happening because we're isolated here?"

"I'm not sure of anything," he admitted, pulling her closer. "All I know now is that if I don't kiss you I'm going to go mad."

The kiss was just a fleeting touch of his lips on hers, but it sent shock waves all the way to her toes. She had been kissed before, but had never experienced her body responding this way. His mouth was warm and gently demanding, the kiss of a man who knew what he was doing and who enjoyed it. His hand moved up under her sweater, but then, to her disappointment, suddenly paused.

"I'm sorry, Charley," he whispered against her throat. "This is not moving slowly."

She was surprised when he got up, but even more surprised when he announced he was going for a walk.

"Zach, that isn't necessary."

"The hell it isn't. I don't want to pressure you. We'll talk in the morning, Charley. Why don't you get some sleep?"

"Sleep," she repeated as she watched him leave the lodge. "You have to be joking, Zach Leighton."

FOURTEEN

You could cut the tension in the kitchen with a knife as they cooked breakfast, neither saying more than a cursory comment as they moved warily around each other.

Charlene had still been awake when Zach had returned to the lodge. She had waited, hoping he would come to her, yet at the same time afraid he would. He hadn't. He had taken a long shower, then crawled into his sleeping bag on the sofa.

She wondered how long she could stand this kind of tension. It was something she'd never experienced, and she felt as if her nerve endings were exposed. Every time she looked at Zach she felt her pulse race. He was so totally male, all hardness and muscles, yet she knew there was also a soft side. How many men cared about things with the passion that he did, and how many men would have taken a walk in the freezing night so she wouldn't feel pressured?

Zach glanced at Charlene. She seemed unusually quiet this morning and he wondered if admitting that he wanted her had scared her. If she didn't feel the sexual tension between them, he wouldn't force the issue, he told himself. He'd just have to continue his walks in sub-zero weather and his cold showers. If she just didn't look so damned cute, and so damned desirable, dressed in her designer jeans with one of his oversize flannel shirts that nearly reached to her knees. Her beautiful blond hair was twisted in one long braid and tied with a string, and she wore the boots that he'd found for her, which only fit when she wore two pairs of his heavy socks. Maybe there was something wrong with him, he thought. How many men would find a woman dressed this way desirable? God, he had to keep his mind on the things that needed to be done around the ranch, he chastised himself. But unfortunately there was too much free time that they would be spending together.

"It snowed again last night," he commented as he dished eggs onto their plate. "It looks like this time I'm going to have to shovel snow off the roofs of the cabins so they won't collapse."

"When does it stop snowing around here?" Charlene asked with a long sigh.

"Maybe May," he answered, glancing at her to see her reaction.

"Oh" was all she said.

"What? No ranting and raving about this godforsaken place?" he asked with a smile.

"No," she said as she poured them coffee. "What good would it do me? I tried to make my escape and almost got myself killed, so I'll just try to enjoy my forced vacation. What is it they say; it does no good to rage against our fate."

Zach laughed. "I didn't realize forbearance came with seclusion."

Charlene had to smile, relieved that the tension had eased and he could joke and tease again. "It isn't just that. I've accepted the fact that I'm a partner in this establishment, so I certainly can't continue to be critical of it. Besides, I've come to appreciate some of the things about it."

"Really? And just what have you come to appreciate?"

Charlene wanted to tell him that it was mainly his company, but she didn't want the tension to begin again, so she simply said, "I enjoy the solitude." The look Zach gave her made her wonder if he could read her mind.

"That's hard to believe, Charley. It wasn't that long ago you told me you'd go crazy being isolated here."

"I know, but I've changed. Granted, I'd enjoy going to lunch at the St. Francis Hotel, or going shopping at Ghirardelli Square, but I'm handling it better than I thought I could."

"You are, Charley, and I'm proud of you. When the snow stops for a couple of days, maybe we can take the snowmobile and ride into Moose for lunch."

Charlene almost choked on her coffee as she laughed. "Oh, that sounds wonderful, Zach. A trip to Moose. Is that some kind of grazing field where they serve grass and straw?"

"No," he feigned annoyance with her. "It's a little town near here, and there is a nice bar and restaurant there called the Garwood Saloon."

"Oh, good," she exclaimed. "I can't tell you how relieved I am to hear that."

Zach grinned at her. "Keep it up, lady, and I won't let you enjoy the surprise I planned for this evening."

"Don't tell me," she teased, "we're going on a shopping trip to Bloomingdale's?"

"Jackson Hole doesn't have a Bloomingdale's," he laughed.

"Then tell me what you're planning," she pleaded.

"Well, you've been whining about wanting a hot tub . . ."

"You bought us a hot tub?" she asked in disbelief.

"No," he sighed with great patience. "When would I have had a chance to do that? I've been isolated on this mountain just like you have. But there is a large copper tub stored in the game room, and I thought I'd put it in front of the wood stove in here and fill it with hot water. You can pretend you're at your club soaking in a Jacuzzi."

Charlene's eyes lit up. "Oh, Zach, that sounds wonderful. If you'll do that for me, I'll help you clean the snow off the cabin roofs."

"No way, Charley," he said, laughing. "I'm not letting you get up there and break your pretty neck."

"It's very nice of you to be concerned, but I have to learn to do things around here, just as you feel you have to share equally in money spent for improvements."

"That's fine to a point, Charley, but I don't want you on the roofs. They're slick and dangerous. All

I need is for you to fall off and be laid up for a couple of weeks.''

"Are you concerned that I wouldn't be able to cook for you?'' she asked, pouting.

Zach gave her a devilish grin. "No, Charley, believe me, that hadn't even crossed my mind.''

Charlene felt her heart skip a beat at the way he was looking at her. His blue eyes sparkled. "What . . . what can I do then?'' she asked, feeling the heat rise to her face.

Zach gave her hand a gentle squeeze before he got up to place his dishes in the sink. "Why don't you go through the cabins and make sure no critters have been in them?'' he suggested. "And while you're doing that, maybe you'll get some ideas for redecorating.''

Charlene picked up her dishes and followed him to the sink. "The decorating part sounds fine, but what kind of critters am I looking for?'' she asked suspiciously.

Zach laughed. "Nothing as big as a bear. Well, maybe I better retract that statement. We do have an occasional black bear who gets into the trash, but they're probably hibernating by now.''

"Probably?''

"Don't worry about a thing,'' he assured with a grin. "I'll be close by with my shovel.'' He took his coat from the peg. "I'm going on out and get started. See you there.''

"I'd prefer it if you had a gun,'' she said, following him to the door.

Zach laughed as he put his coat on. "Don't believe in them, Charley.''

* * *

Charlene wandered through the cabins. Each one had a living room, with a very small kitchen area, two bedrooms, and a bath. The living rooms had a fireplace, and a large picture window that overlooked the Tetons but had been boarded up for the winter. Not too bad, she thought, but they definitely could use some new furniture. Everything was wood and plaid.

She didn't look too hard for critters, afraid she might find one, but she did discover that water had been left dripping in all the bathrooms. "What a waste," she murmured as she made sure each spigot was turned off.

When she had checked all the cabins, she followed the wooden pathway that Zach had already cleared, and found him on the roof of the next to last cabin. "Hi!" she shouted.

"Hi, yourself." He paused for a moment and smiled down at her. "Find any critters?"

"No sign of anything."

"Good. I've got one more cabin after this one, so if you want to go back to the lodge, go ahead."

"I think I'll just hang around for a while and watch you."

"OK. I'll work fast."

Charlene enjoyed watching him. She'd never paid much attention to men doing physical labor, but if they all looked as good as Zach Leighton, she'd have to start paying more attention. "Zach, you said something earlier about a game room. Where is that?"

"It's off the main room of the lodge, princess. Haven't you noticed the double doors leading off both sides of the room? There's a dining room off one side and a game room off the other."

"I thought the doors were closets," she admitted sheepishly. "What's in the game room?"

"A couple of card tables, a bar, and a pool table."

"A pool table," she repeated.

"Yeah," he said with a grin. "That's a game where you use a stick to hit little balls into pockets. If you'd like to learn I'll be glad to teach you."

Charlene smiled, thinking how many times she'd spent the evening playing pool at the club. It was one of the few games she was really good at. "I've never been very good at games," she answered, tongue in cheek, "but maybe I'll do better at pool than I've done at poker."

"I haven't given up on you learning to be a good poker player, Charley. As a matter of fact, I thought the next time we played, I'd teach you to play strip poker. It might be easier for you."

"Whatever you say, cowboy," Charlene said, tossing a snowball at him.

"Hey, watch it," he laughed.

"I want you to know I saved us a lot of money, Mr. Leighton," she said smugly.

"Really? How is that, princess?" Zach asked as he continued to shovel.

"You're lucky I'm observant."

"Observant? You just said you thought the dining room and game room were closets."

"Zach, I'm serious," she said petulantly.

"Sorry, Charley. Tell me how you saved us money."

"I discovered leaking faucets in every cabin, but I turned them all off," she announced proudly.

"You did what?" Zach shouted.

"I said, faucets were leaking," she shouted up to him, thinking he was having trouble hearing her, "and I turned them all off."

"For God's sake, woman, what are you trying to do to me?" he screamed, throwing his shovel off the roof. "If the faucets aren't dripping, the pipes will freeze. I can't believe this . . ."

"Zach, calm down before you . . ."

Before she could finish what she was about to say, Zach began to slide toward the edge. With the shovel on the ground, there was nothing he could use to dig in. She watched horrified as he struggled to grab ahold of something, but to no avail. "Zach . . . oh, God, Zach," she screamed as he fell off the roof.

Fortunately he fell into a pile of snow he had just finished scooping off the roof. It broke the worst of his fall, but he knew right away that he'd hurt his leg. He closed his eyes and grimaced against the pain.

"Zach, Zach, speak to me," Charlene pleaded, kneeling beside him. She placed her hands gently on his face, almost afraid to touch him. "Please, tell me you're not dead."

Zach opened his eyes and stared at her. She looked so concerned, and so damned beautiful leaning over him. His anger instantly evaporated, and instead of screaming at her, he pulled her head down to meet his lips, kissing her long and languorously. When he released her he smiled. "I'm not dead, princess, but you may be if the pipes freeze."

"I didn't know, Zach," she said breathlessly. "I'm sorry. I'll take care of it. Just tell me you're all right."

Zach struggled to sit up, stretching his arms and legs. "Damn," he hissed.

"What is it? What hurts?"

"I twisted my bad knee."

"Don't worry about a thing," she assured him. "I'll get you back to the lodge and take care of everything."

Suddenly Zach laughed. "Calm down, Charley. I'm not an invalid. All I need is a shoulder to lean on. I'll use ice and heat on the knee the rest of the day, and by tomorrow I should be back on my feet."

"I hope you will be, but don't worry if you're not up to it. I'll take care of everything. I can bring wood in, and even shovel off the roofs if I have to," she assured him as they slowly made their way to the lodge. "First thing I'll do is get you an ice pack, then I'll turn the faucets back on in the cabins, and then I'll fix you a dinner you won't forget . . ."

Zach stopped walking and pulled her around to face him. "Charley, I won't ever be able to forget anything you do," he said, grinning down at her. "You're a surprise a minute, but just calm down. I'm fine."

Charlene stared at him, her green eyes filled with concern. "I was so afraid . . ."

"Thanks for being concerned," he whispered as his lips met hers, his tongue probing the soft sweetness of her mouth, gently at first, then more demanding. She melted against him, even though she held his weight. She moaned softly as he lifted his head. "I want you, Charley."

She stared back at him, with sultry sea-green eyes trying to gather her senses. "You're hurt, Zach. This isn't the time," she whispered.

"You're damn right I'm hurting, Charley, but it isn't from the fall," he admitted softly.

She took a deep breath and turned sideways, pulling his arm over her shoulder again so they could continue their arduous task of getting to the lodge. "You must have fallen on your head, Zach Leighton," she said, trying to make her voice sound stern. "You can't even walk and here you are talking about getting me into your bed."

Zach grinned down at her. "I was thinking more along the lines of getting into *your* bed. That couch is mighty small for the two of us, Charley."

Charlene adopted an attitude of being in charge, yet she felt anything but in charge. Her knees were weak and her mouth felt as if she had cotton in it. Why should this man affect her this way? she wondered uneasily. "Maybe you'd better wait until I finish playing doctor before you decide if you want me or not," she warned.

"Oh, no," he laughed. "That warning sounds very ominous, princess, but really, all I need is an ice pack."

"Now, you wouldn't deny me the pleasure of playing doctor, would you?" she asked with a wicked gleam in her eyes. "I used to operate on all my dollies."

"You know, Charley, suddenly my leg feels better."

"Don't be afraid, cowboy," she teased. "I promise not to hurt you too bad. I'm really a whiz at taking stitches."

"Oh, no," Zach moaned. "What have I gotten myself into?"

FIFTEEN

Propped up in bed, Zach studied Charlene as she placed the ice pack on his knee. "I could do that for myself," he commented, "but I have to admit, it wouldn't be half as nice as having you do it."

"Don't get too spoiled, Zach Leighton. You did promise you'd be fine tomorrow, and my guilt only lasts twenty-four hours," she teased. "Now, here," she said, handing him a glass of water, "I want you to take two aspirin."

"Yes, ma'am. Whatever you say," he answered with a grin. "Anything to keep you from performing surgery on my knee."

"That isn't out of the question yet," she warned. "Now, why don't you rest for a while while I correct my mistake at the cabins."

"All right, Charley, but you be careful. Stay away from wolves and bears."

"Very funny, Leighton," she said, giving him a scathing look.

"You just let the faucets barely drip," he instructed, "but there does have to be a steady drip."

"I understand," she said, putting her fur coat on. "If you're not back in thirty minutes I'm coming to get you."

"Don't you dare, Zach Leighton. I'll be back as soon as I finish the job. I want you to stay off that leg because I don't want to have to play nursemaid to you."

Zach laughed. "My God, now my words are coming back to haunt me. What next?"

"What next, indeed," she said, a twinkle in her green eyes as she left the lodge.

Zach smiled as he leaned back against the pillows. He was probably making the biggest mistake in his life, but he was on the brink of becoming lovers with his partner. Where it went from there he didn't know, but he knew without a doubt that he had to proceed. They had been playing this cat-and-mouse game long enough, he decided. To hell with common sense. He wanted her and he was certain she wanted him.

Charlene wandered through the first cabin mumbling to herself. What in the world was wrong with her? She was feeling like a love-starved teenager. True, Zach Leighton was handsome and had the power to twist her insides into knots like no man had ever done, but she had to stay in control of her emotions. "Sure, you can stay in control until you're in the same room with him again," she chastised herself out loud. Just thinking about him made her weak and shaky. Whatever possessed her? she wondered, feeling the heat rise in her body. She couldn't ever remember thinking about a man this way, but then, Zach Leighton wasn't just any man. He was special, very special. If she gave in to this desire for him, would there ever be more between them than just sex? She barely knew Zach, and he knew very little about her. No. That wasn't true. They'd only been together a short time, but he probably knew more about her than any other person, including her mother.

Charlene stared at the dripping water. Maybe she was agonizing over something that would never happen. She thought Zach desired her, but she wasn't certain. It was possible that flirting and teasing were just his way. She took a deep breath to steady her nerves. She'd just have to take things as they came, she decided.

With that decided, she quickly went through the cabins, adjusting all the faucets, then headed back to the lodge. Zach had fallen asleep, his pants leg still rolled up and the ice bag still on his knee. She stared at him, her eyes wandering over his face. His nose and cheekbones looked as if they had been chiseled by a master sculptor, yet at the same time, there was a ruggedness to his handsome face. It was the kind of face women drooled over and men envied. He had fine lines that fanned out from his blue eyes; laugh lines, she had once heard someone call them. She touched the corners of her own eyes. There wasn't a chance she had laugh lines—not yet, anyway, she smiled. If she stayed around Zach Leighton long enough she'd surely have them.

Lifting the ice pack off his knee, she was distressed to find it was terribly swollen. She wondered if she should let him sleep, or start alternating the ice with heat. Finally she decided it was better for him to sleep, and she headed for the kitchen to decide what to cook for them. This would be her first meal totally on her own, and she wanted it to be special.

Searching through the freezer, she found containers marked "spaghetti with meatballs." Apparently the ranch's chef had prepared them for Zach. As many as they were, they must be one of his favorites, she decided. "Let's see, the club always served salad and garlic bread with spaghetti," she mumbled, searching through the refrigerator for something to make a green salad. The lettuce she found was in terrible shape, but after picking through it, she decided she had enough for two salads. She placed it in cold water, hoping it would revive. The only other things she could find to add were olives, cheese, and onions. She didn't imagine Zach had salads once the snows started, since produce would be impossible to store for long.

After glancing through the cookbook to find out how to make garlic bread, she decided she was all set to fix dinner. "Now what?" she wondered, rubbing her hands together. She'd better add logs to the wood stove and fireplace. She didn't want Zach to think she couldn't take care of things while he was recuperating.

When that was done, a brilliant idea hit her. Zach had planned to put the copper tub in front of the wood stove for her this evening. She would just turn the tables on him. It would probably do his knee a world of good. She filled every large kettle she could find with water and put them on the stove to heat. The next thing she had to do was get the copper tub from the game room to the kitchen without waking Zach.

The game room was much nicer than she'd expected. She stood in the center of the room taking everything in. There was a large gray stone fireplace in the corner of the room, and lots of paintings on the log walls. Each green felt-covered card table had a Tiffany-style lamp over it, and the beautiful ornate pool table had a long brass lamp above it. She ran her hand along the wood of the pool table, thinking it must be very old, even though it was in beautiful shape. The bar was also wood-and-brass, with four stools in front of it. Then she noticed an artist's easel in the corner. It held an unfinished painting of a wolf standing on a rock silhouetted by the moon. It was absolutely beautiful, she thought as she studied it. Suddenly she remembered Zach having mentioned that he spent his time reading, listening to music, and painting. This was the first time she had thought about it. If this was his work, he had real talent. She studied one of the beautiful paintings of wildflowers on the wall and discovered a small "zl" in the lower corner. Examining the rest of the paintings, she found the same initials on each one. Zach Leighton was good enough to have a showing in an art gallery, she thought.

Suddenly she shivered. Without a fire in the fireplace, the room was freezing. Where was the tub? she wondered. Opening a door, she found a well-stocked closet full of glasses, towels, and various games, but no tub. She was about to give up when she spotted something gleaming behind the bar. Tugging at the tub, it slowly moved. She was never going to be able to get it into the kitchen this way, she thought. It had handles, but it was too heavy for her to pick up. She was going to have to drag it, but how without waking Zach? Taking several towels from the closet, she placed them under one end of the tub, then lifted the other end by the handle and began to drag it silently across the wooden floor.

She glanced at Zach as she passed through the great room and was relieved to see he was still sleeping like a baby. Once she made it to the kitchen, she struggled under the weight of each kettle of boiling water to pour them into the tub. She then refilled the kettles and placed them back on the stove, deciding four more kettles of hot water and then enough cold water to get the temperature just right should do it.

"What are you up to, Charley?" Zach asked, leaning against the doorway.

Charlene jumped at the sound of his voice. "What are you doing out of bed? You're supposed to be sleeping."

"I saw you creeping past me with that tub and my curiosity got the best of me. Are you getting ready to take a bath?"

"No. I was preparing it for you. I thought a hot soak would help your knee."

"That's real sweet of you, princess, but I know you were looking forward to soaking in it. I'm just sorry I wasn't able to prepare it for you."

"Zach, let me do this for you. I've never done anything special for anyone," she admitted, "and I've enjoyed planning this surprise."

Zach smiled. "How can I refuse when you put it that way?"

"Good. I'll use the tub tomorrow evening."

He gave her a wicked grin. "There is a solution, Charley. We could enjoy it together."

"Get in the tub, Leighton," she ordered with a laugh, dismissing his suggestion.

"OK, Doc," he agreed, his hand going to his belt, while watching her face.

A pink blush rose to her cheeks, just as he knew it would. "For heaven's sake, let me get out of here first," she exclaimed, flustered.

"I may need your help."

"Ha. You made it in here without me, cowboy, and I'm sure you can make it into the tub without me."

"What if the water is too hot?"

"Check it before you undress," she said patiently, "and I'll adjust it for you."

"You have an answer for everything, Charley," he said, amusement in his voice. "I tell you what. There's a privacy screen in the dining room. You could put it in front of the tub and that way you could at least stay in here with me. I wouldn't want to drown and you not hear me."

Charlene pretended to be annoyed. "I may drown you myself, Leighton. The water is going to be cold before you get into it."

When Charlene returned with the screen, Zach had his shoes and socks and shirt off. She stood staring at him for a long moment. She had seen his torso from the back, but now she was exposed to a broad, hard-muscled chest with a light smattering of dark hair. She gasped as she noticed for the first time that he had a jagged scar along his left side.

"Is something wrong, Charley?"

"Where did you get that terrible scar?" she asked

in a breathless voice. "It looks like something tore you open."

"It did," he said with a bitter laugh. "I zigged when I should have zagged, and the Brahma bull I was sparring with won."

Charlene moved slowly toward him, as if drawn to him. All she could think about was what pain he must have suffered. He stood stock-still as she touched the scar, running her finger along the raised skin. "It must have hurt terribly."

"It did," he answered softly, not wanting to break the spell, "But it was a long time ago." Her gentle touch sent a hot, rippling sensation through him. His eyes were drawn to her soft pink lips. Swallowing hard, he tried to control his desire, but there was no way. He folded her into his arms, his lips feather-soft against her throat. "You smell wonderful, like an exotic flower."

She tensed as he ran his tongue around her ear. "Zach," she moaned.

His mouth came down on hers, demanding, possessing. When he lifted his head, she quickly stepped backward, trying to keep from falling to her knees. "Your bath . . ." There was an edge of panic in her voice.

Zach took a deep breath, trying to compose himself. "You're hell on my nerves, lady," he finally managed to say with a bittersweet laugh.

"I'm sorry," she said, tears filling her eyes. "I'm not very good at this." She turned away from him, unable to bear the pained expression on his face. "I'm afraid, Zach."

"You have nothing to be afraid of, Charley," he said, his voice soft and reassuring.

She wanted to tell him she was afraid she was falling in love with him, and she knew she would end up being hurt. Sooner or later she would have to go back to San Francisco and he would stay in Wyoming, and they would have to settle for a long-distance relationship, or no relationship at all. Turning back, she forced a smile. "Haven't you ever heard that those who do not learn from history are condemned to repeat it? Get in your bath, cowboy. I have to start dinner."

He knew she was referring to her mother and Cody's failure at their relationship. "Maybe we're smarter, Charley."

"What if we're not?" she asked, tears brimming in her eyes.

"Life's a gamble, sweetheart. You have to take chances."

Charlene laughed nervously. "I told you my grandmother warned me about gambling. Now, get in your bath before it's cold," she ordered. "I have to start dinner."

Charlene quickly set up the screen, then disappeared on the other side of it. She gripped the countertop, trying to still her nerves and her breathing.

She heard the water splash as Zach lowered himself into the tub, and her imagination jumped full steam ahead, not helping the situation a bit.

"Charley," he called softly.

"Yes?" she answered after a moment's hesitation.

"You're a coward," he accused, humor in his voice.

"I know," she answered.

"This isn't over, Charley. Don't make me wait

too long before you admit you want me as much as I want you.''

She was silent, unsure what to say. She did want him. Why couldn't she just relax and let it happen? *Tell him you want him*, a little voice prodded. ''Zach . . .''

''Yeah, Charley?''

She swallowed with difficulty before speaking. ''Is spaghetti and meatballs all right with you?''

Zach's laughter surprised her. ''You're going to drive me crazy, woman, but I'll say one thing, our time together certainly hasn't been boring.''

SIXTEEN

Charlene listened to Zach whistle as he scrubbed. Smiling, she took a box of spaghetti from the pantry.

"The water is perfect, Charley. Are you sure you won't join me?"

Charlene swallowed hard before answering. "Thanks, Zach, but I think I'll wait until tomorrow night to enjoy my bath." She tried to concentrate on reading the directions on the side of the box, but all she could think about was him naked on the other side of the screen.

He was now humming a tune, then there was a thump. "Charlene, I need your help. I dropped the soap."

"Zach . . ." she said with a moan.

"Come on, Charley, have a heart. It was hard enough to get in here without assistance. There's no way I can get out to get my soap. Please . . ."

"All right," she agreed with a shiver of anticipation. "Just stay in the water."

Charlene approached the screen, taking a deep breath. "You're mighty clumsy, cowboy."

"Yeah, I know," he smiled as her eyes met his. "I'll have to try to be more careful."

Picking the soap up, Charlene held it out to him, trying not to look anyplace but his face. "Don't lose it again," she warned, "because I'm getting ready to fix dinner and I can't be running back here to retrieve your soap every few minutes."

Zach held out his hand, but instead of taking the soap, he grabbed her by the wrist and pulled her into the tub.

"Zach!" she screamed, then began to laugh. "Oh, God, look what you've done to me. My clothes are ruined."

He gave a wicked laugh. "You should see what you've done to me, princess."

Suddenly she realized it was time to come to a decision. She stared up into his blue eyes, wanting some kind of assurance. "Zach, are you sure this is the right thing to do?"

"I've never been surer of anything in my life, Charley," he answered, his voice a husky murmur.

"We're moving so fast," she protested feebly.

"Honey, I want you, and I think you want me. Stop thinking with your head and let your heart tell you what to do." Wrapping his hand in her hair, he forced her mouth to meet his. Charlene moaned as his warm lips moved against her mouth, nibbling and teasing before his tongue found its way inside to savor and explore. She might as well be a virgin, she thought mindlessly. No man had ever had this kind of an effect on her. She trembled under his touch as a fever began to rage through her body. He was right about one thing: every fiber of her being wanted him.

His hand moved up under her wet shirt, drifted over her ribs, then gently caressed her breasts. "You feel so good," he moaned soft and low, trying to shift her weight so that she sat on him.

She saw him grimace in pain when her weight settled on his leg. "Zach, your knee," she whispered, concern in her voice.

"I'd like nothing better than to take you here and now, princess, but maybe it would be better if we got out of this tub. I want to be able to savor every inch of you, and that's a little difficult in such close quarters."

Charlene giggled as she struggled to lift herself out of the tub without hurting his leg. "Are you sure you're up to doing this?"

He smiled again, a virile, wicked grin that touched one corner of his mouth. "Believe me, I'm *up* to it, princess. I'll prove it to you in a few minutes."

Charlene laughed softly as she offered him her hand. "You're a wicked man, Zach Leighton," she said in a raspy voice as she stared at his beautiful body. "I believe you're trying to corrupt me."

Zach laughed seductively as he wrapped a towel around his waist. "Ah, sweetness, didn't you know the devil makes wickedness attractive so he can corrupt the innocent?"

"I believe it," she said, smiling up at him. "Lean on me and I'll help you into the other room."

When they reached the bed, he sat down on the side but didn't let go of her. "Take those wet things off, Charley," he growled.

"Maybe I should go into the bathroom . . ."

"No. I want to watch you."

A shiver of anticipation trickled down her spine. She had never done anything like this, yet she found herself responding by slowly unbuttoning her shirt.

Zach noticed the flush of her skin. "Does undressing in front of me embarrass you, honey?"

Charlene shrugged her shoulders. "It's just that I've never been naked in front of a man before," she admitted shyly.

Zach gently pulled her onto his lap, nuzzling the side of her throat. "You said you had been with a man before."

"It wasn't anything like this . . . like what I feel with you." She stammered over her words. "It was over faster than it takes you to kiss me." Charlene took a deep breath before going on. "I didn't even undress. We were in the backseat of a car, and . . . he just . . . raised my skirt," she finally managed to get out. Closing her eyes, she tried to block out the memory. "I had had too much to drink, but even that didn't disguise the fact that it was terrible."

Zach swore softly. The thought of anyone using her that way made him furious. If he had the bastard there, he'd probably kill him. "I'm sorry, baby," he said, holding her close against his strong body. "Any man in his right mind would have made your first time special for you. All it takes is a little patience on the man's part."

"I don't want to think about it," she whispered, clinging to him. "I only know that it's different with you. You make me feel special by just wanting me."

He kissed the tender skin along her jawline, then moved slowly down her throat. "Put that experience from your mind, Charley. *This* is your first time with a man. I'm going to show you how a man can make you feel like a woman who is desired and loved."

Charlene closed her eyes as she felt him undo her bra. Zach Leighton had already made her feel desired and special. "Wait," she said as he started to undo her jeans. She stood up and slipped her boots and socks off, then slowly inched her jeans and lacy underwear down over her hips, her eyes holding his.

"You are so beautiful," he whispered as his eyes lingered on her perfect body. "I'm glad no one has ever seen you before, princess. Your body is for my eyes only," he said, running his hands down her sides and over her slim hips.

Charlene felt tears running down her face. Her body was for his eyes only, but for how long? When the time came that she could get off the mountain, would he want her to go? Oh, God, she couldn't bear to think of that now. It didn't matter what the future held. Only this moment mattered. This had to be right, because nothing that felt this good could be wrong.

She sighed softly as he pulled her down on the bed to lie beside him. His tongue gently touched her breast, tracing a moist circle around one nipple, then the other. She never imagined experiencing the feelings he elicited with his mouth. Her fingers grasped his hair, holding his head to her. "Your skin feels like velvet," he whispered, his breath warm against her flesh.

Her response was blind emotion as she lifted her hips off the bed, wanting something more, something to relieve the ache that was building inside her.

"Not yet, sweetheart," he whispered as his hand

explored between her legs. "This time it is going to be perfect for you, a time you'll never forget."

His fingers caressed and explored her most intimate place, and she was certain she'd go out of her mind with wanting him. Tentatively, she moved her hand down over his hard-muscled stomach, wanting him to feel what she was feeling, but not sure how to go about it. Feeling him tense and hearing his breath catch, she stopped, wondering if her touch was painful to him.

"Don't stop, honey. That feels wonderful."

"I want to know how to please you," she whispered against his mouth. "The things you're doing to me make me feel so good."

Zach ran his tongue over her lips. "The same things that make you feel good make me feel good," he whispered, his breath mingling with her. "Just lying next to you makes me feel like I could lose my mind loving you."

"I want you so bad, Zach," she moaned, placing little nibbling kisses along his mouth. "I want you to take me now, please."

He had wanted to go slow, to draw this out until she couldn't stand it, but her words nearly made him lose control. His knee screamed pain as he tried to shift his weight to be closer to her. "We're going to have to be a little unorthodox in the way we do this, sweetheart."

"You're in pain, aren't you?" she asked, concern mixed with desire in her sea-green eyes.

"It's nothing that we can't work around," he assured her as he rolled onto his back. He leaned over and took something off the table next to the bed. She closed her eyes, realizing he had thought to have protection nearby. "Straddle me, sweetheart," he instructed a moment later. When Charlene did what he told her, he lifted her hips and slowly lowered her on his staff.

She closed her eyes and threw her head back, certain that she would die from the pleasure. Her moans filled the quiet room.

He drove into her, filling her. She was tight against him, tight yet moist, and he felt he'd never had a woman fit him so perfectly. With his hands on her hips he raised and lowered her the first couple of times, but then she began a natural rocking motion. "That's it, sweetheart, take everything I have to give you. Don't hold back," he said between gritted teeth as he tried to control his own climax.

"Zach . . ." Her eyes flew open as the flames began to consume her. "Oh, God, Zach." Each deep thrust sent fire rushing through her body. She felt consumed with the sensations.

"That's it, honey," he responded, his breathing ragged as he finally let go, his body stiffening as he strained to drive even deeper.

When he gave a final thrust, he pulled her down to lie on top of him, still buried deep inside her. He captured her mouth once more with a sweet, gentle kiss. "My God, woman, I thought you were going to set this bed on fire," he said breathlessly.

She smiled at him, pleased with herself and feeling totally satiated. "I thought you were going to set this mountain on fire. I was afraid we were both going to go up in flames."

"This was just the beginning," he said with a boyish grin that made her heart ache with love. "Wait until my knee is better."

"You're very cocky, cowboy," she said as she stroked his face lovingly, "but I suppose you have a right to be."

His chuckle was low and sexy. "That's the nicest thing you could have said, Charley. A man always likes to know when he pleases a woman."

Charlene's smile faded as she stared into his eyes. "You please me, Zach Leighton. Oh, God, how you please me," she admitted, tears brimming from her eyes.

"Baby, what's the matter?" he asked, pulling her tightly against his chest.

She managed a laugh though she was sniffling. "I'm just happy. You make me feel so cherished and safe."

Zach closed his eyes as he stroked her hair. *How long will you let me make you feel that way, love?* he wondered silently. *When the weather eases, will you pack your bags and just say goodbye?* It didn't matter, he told himself. He wouldn't trade the last half hour for anything in the world. If it had to be just a memory to hold on to, then so be it. He'd known it was a mistake to fall in love with her, but somehow common sense had taken a backseat to emotions.

SEVENTEEN

Zach stood at the side of the bed sipping his coffee as he gazed at the sleeping beauty still curled up under the quilts. She was so beautiful lying there, her blond hair all tousled around her flushed face. It felt right having her there, he thought. She had insisted on fixing them a late dinner, but they had ended up in bed again after that, making love into the early hours of the morning. Just thinking about it made his body stir with desire.

It was strange, he'd never felt so closely tuned to anyone before, yet what did they have in common except for the partnership in this ranch?

Zach shook his head in disgust at himself. There he was thinking they had to have something in common again. He and Monica had many things in common, but that hadn't worked out. He told Charley to stop thinking with her head and follow her heart, but why was he having so much trouble following his own advice? Was it still the fear that she would leave the first opportunity she had? That wasn't just a possibility, it was a fact. She was a Van Payton and was expected to take over the family business, but where did that leave him? There was no way he'd do what Cody had attempted to do; give up everything to try to live in her world. No, his time with Charley would mean no commitments, no happily ever after, he thought sadly. He'd have to enjoy and savor their time from one moment to the next.

He sat down on the edge of the bed and ran his hand over her derriere that was provocatively outlined under the quilts. "Wake up, sleeping beauty." Charlene mumbled something he couldn't understand and buried deeper under the covers. "Come on, sweetheart, you have roofs to clean, breakfast to make, and wood to chop . . ."

Charlene threw the quilts off her head and glared at him. "What did you say?"

A teasing smile covered his handsome face. "You did say yesterday that you'd take care of everything, since I am an invalid."

Charlene giggled, pulling the quilts back over her head. "You blew your invalid status last night, cowboy. No one in this world knows better than me how fit you are."

"Is that right?" He laughed, tickling her. "Am I to assume then that you enjoyed last night?"

Charlene smiled, remembering with delicious clarity how wonderful their lovemaking had been. Zach had been a wild, passionate lover, and had satisfied her in ways she'd never known a woman could be satisfied. After her only other encounter with sex, she had considered it grossly overrated, and had even considered celibacy for the rest of her life, but now she knew better, thanks to Zach's expertise.

"I'm waiting, Charley," he said softly, his blue eyes warm and promising. "Did you enjoy last night?"

"What is this, Leighton, an ego trip?" she asked, trying to keep a straight face. "Last night was a nice way to spend an evening when you're bored out of your mind."

"Oh, is that right?" he asked, amusement in his sultry eyes. "So the only reason you enjoyed it is because there was nothing else to do."

"Something like that," she answered, trying to keep from laughing.

A strangled sound came out of his throat as he grabbed her and pulled her into his arms, tickling her until she was exhausted with laughter. "I think I'm going to have to teach you a lesson, you little vixen. I'm going to do things to you that you never imagined, I'm going to make you beg me to bring you to release, and then I'm going to . . ."

Suddenly her laughter ceased as the movement of his hands changed from tickling to tenderly exploring. "I was just teasing you," she whispered. "You were wonderful and I have never enjoyed anything as much as I did your lovemaking."

Zach kissed her long and passionately, savoring the moment before lifting his head to stare into her eyes. "I knew you enjoyed it," he said smugly. "I have the scars to prove it."

"Don't blame me for your scars," she said, placing a kiss on the scar that marred his side. "A bull did this to you."

Zach snickered. "I'm talking about the scars on

my back. I was thinking I might have to let you practice your stitching technique on me after all.''

Charlene lifted her head and stared at him. ''Zach, what are you talking about?''

''You were a tiger, Charley, a wild woman. A woman doesn't react like that unless she is enjoying the act,'' he said with a knowing grin.

''Turn over and let me see your back,'' she ordered, still not believing him.

''Oh, God!'' she exclaimed, seeing her nail marks in red streaks down his flesh. ''I did this? Oh, my God, I don't know what got into me. I'm so sorry, Zach. Does it hurt bad? I should use an antiseptic on these welts and maybe . . .''

''Charley, calm down,'' he laughed as he turned over on his back and pulled her on top of him.

''Zach, this is serious! I lost control, don't you understand that?''

''You bet I do, princess. If you had asked me my name last night I wouldn't have been able to tell you. It was exactly the way it should be, the way every man and woman fantasizes it will be,'' he reassured her, wrapping his hand in her tangled mass of hair. ''These scratches are nothing,'' he said, placing a tender kiss on her lips. ''I was just teasing you because I enjoyed it so much, and I knew you did, too.''

''Doesn't it hurt?'' she asked, her green eyes still filled with concern.

''Not a bit,'' he growled as he nibbled on her lower lip. ''You can turn into a wildcat with me anytime you want, sweetheart.''

''Oh, God, I may never have sex again. I might

really do you bodily harm the next time," she moaned, completely serious.

Zach laughed as he rolled over on top of her, pinning her with his leg. "That's what you think, princess. You're addictive, and I have no intention of letting you get away from me. Besides, what's a scratch or a bite or two between friends?" he teased.

Her eyes widened in disbelief. "I bit you, too?"

"No, not yet, but there's always the next time."

"Oh, Zach," she finally laughed as she snuggled against him. "Am I really addictive?"

Zach gave an exaggerated sigh. "I knew I shouldn't have said that. Now you'll probably make me do all the cleaning and cooking in exchange for your favors."

"That's a thought." She smiled at him as she ran her long fingernail over his lips. "Ummm, is that coffee I smell?" she said, sniffing the air.

Zach laughed. "How can you think of coffee at a time like this?"

"Zach," she drawled, amusement in her dancing eyes. "If we're going to continue at this pace, I'm going to have to have sustenance."

He smiled, nuzzling the side of her throat. "I was hoping dinner last night would last you a few days."

Laughing, Charlene pushed herself off of him. "Not at the pace you go, cowboy. I might have to call in for intravenous feedings."

"Damn," he swore as he sat up on the side of the bed. "I must have lost my irresistible Leighton charm when a woman who has just spent the night in bed with me prefers food to my lovemaking."

"Zach," she laughed, tenderness in her voice.

"You are the most wonderful, sexy man in the world, but I still have to have food."

"All right, all right." He pretended exasperation. "If it's sustenance you require, I suppose I better provide it. How about French toast and bacon?"

"Oh, that sounds wonderful," she said, licking her lips as she pulled his flannel robe on. "Do you mind if I take a shower while you prepare breakfast? I promise to fix dinner this evening."

Charlene stood under the hot water, letting it cascade over her. Her skin felt warm and sensitive, and there was a delicious ache between her legs. Last night had been the most wonderful experience of her life. She realized her life had meant nothing until she met Zach Leighton, and she didn't know how she would ever walk away from him. A knock at the bathroom door startled her out of her thoughts.

"Hey, you want a cup of coffee in there?" Zach shouted from the other side of the door.

Charlene smiled, feeling warm all over. "That would be wonderful," she said, turning off the water. "You are so considerate."

Zach was leaning against the doorframe, a smile on his handsome face. "I had selfish reasons, princess. I was missing you, and hoped to get a glimpse of that beautiful body before you put clothes on."

Color streaked her cheekbones as she stepped from the shower, yet she didn't hurry to wrap the towel around her. Her eyes met his, and the smile she gave him was filled with love. "You make me feel so special," she said in a low voice.

"You *are* special, sweetheart," he said, giving her a quick kiss, "and if I didn't have bacon on the stove I'd show you just how special I think you are. Now hurry up and get dressed. I'm ready to start the French toast."

Charlene giggled as he lightly smacked her on the bottom. "I'll be right there."

After breakfast they washed dishes together, discussing what they'd do for the afternoon. "You said you'd teach me to play pool," Charlene mentioned, "and we still haven't had that snowmobile ride."

"We could do both, Charley," he replied as he put the dishes up in the cupboard. "I'll do whatever it takes to keep you happy."

Charlene laughed delightedly. "Decisions, decisions."

Zach captured her between his strong arms, pinning her against the sink. He lifted her hair and kissed the back of her neck, then made patterns with his moist tongue beneath her ear until she moaned. "I said you were addictive, sweetheart, but don't get it in your mind to torture me."

Charlene turned around and wrapped her arms around his neck. "I wouldn't think of it," she said breathlessly as she drew his head down to her mouth. The taste of him was like a fine wine, making her feel dizzy and giddy.

With aching slowness, he moved his hand up under her shirt to gently cup her breast. He felt the nipple instantly grow hard against his hand. "I think you're as addicted as I am."

"I think you're right," she admitted, her face instantly flushed with yearning. The feel of his calloused hands was rough against her tender skin, making her feel as if every nerve ending was exposed. It was a feeling that sent a current from her brain to her toes, pulsating through every inch of her body. "Zach," she moaned. "What are we going to do about it?"

His smile was slow and lazy, and completely disarming. "Well, for starters we're not going to play pool," he whispered, rotating his hips against her, leaving no doubt what he had in mind.

"Or go for a snowmobile ride," she whispered brokenly.

EIGHTEEN

"I think I could learn to like this lovemaking," she whispered against his shoulder.

Zach laughed deep in his throat. "I think I'm going to need to take some vitamins if we keep this up."

Charlene giggled. "You started this, Leighton. I was perfectly content to go for a snowmobile ride."

"I know you were," he said, kissing her temple, "but even with the beautiful scenery around here, it wouldn't have been half as enjoyable as making love to you."

Charlene leaned up on her elbow. "Speaking of scenery, you are quite an artist, Zach Leighton. Why didn't you tell me you'd painted all the pictures around here?"

Zach smiled. "The subject never came up, sweetheart."

"I absolutely love the painting of the wolf that you're working on. It's incredibly beautiful, and since I've come face-to-face with one of those creatures, I know exactly how realistic it is.''

"I'm glad you like it. When I finish it, it's yours.'' *Something to remember me by,* he thought silently.

"I would love that,'' she smiled tenderly, running her hand over his chest. "You know, you're good enough to have your own showing at an art gallery.''

"That's nice of you to say, Charley, but I paint mostly for my own enjoyment. Occasionally I sell a few paintings at one of the art galleries in town.''

"There is an art gallery in Jackson Hole?'' she asked in disbelief.

"Honey, for your information, we're not all that far behind your cosmopolitan San Francisco. Most people think Jackson Hole is just wilderness and mountains, but when you finally get tired of staring at the beauty and grandeur of the Tetons, which a lot of people never do, you'll find Jackson Hole has a blend of culture and sophistication along with its rugged outdoor activities. We have several fine arts and crafts galleries, several first-rate museums, two live summer theaters, an excellent library, two well-edited newspapers, and a beautifully produced local magazine is published here. You can also attend a rodeo at one end of town, and a summer symphony performing Mozart at the other.''

"I didn't know,'' she mused, wondering if she could be happy there. She knew one thing for sure, she would never be happy away from Zach.

"What are you thinking about?'' he asked, running his hand up and down her arm.

"I was just thinking about your paintings. Are

there really fields and valleys of wildflowers like you painted?"

"There sure are. It's one of the most beautiful sights you'll ever see. Wyoming's state flower is the Indian paintbrush, a vivid red flower that covers the hillsides in the summer. There are people who come here just to enjoy the wildflowers."

"It sounds beautiful."

Zach studied her face, wondering if he dare ask her if she could live there. What the hell, he thought. He wouldn't know until he asked. "Charley, do you think you could . . ."

The foreign sound of the telephone ring interrupted what he was about to ask.

"My heavens." Charlene jumped. "I almost forgot you had a telephone."

Zach climbed from the bed and wrapped a towel around his waist. "It's times like this I wish I didn't," he growled before answering it.

Charlene laid back against the pillows and studied Zach. She was thinking he was so masculine and sinfully handsome when she realized he was signaling her to come to the phone.

"Just a moment," he was saying.

Charlene gripped the sheet, her eyes wide with apprehension.

"I believe it's your mother," he said shortly.

Charlene swallowed, wrapping the sheet around her as she climbed from the bed. Somehow it didn't seem right to be naked with your lover when your mother was on the phone.

"Hello," she said tentatively.

"Hello, dear. I was getting a little concerned about

you since you sounded so distressed during our last phone conversation.''

''It's nice to know you care,'' she said, her eyes darting back to Zach.

''I thought you'd be calling me back before now, dear. It's been two weeks.''

''Has it?'' Charlene asked as she watched Zach pull his pants on.

''Are you all right, dear?''

''Yes, I'm fine. As I told you, I'm snowed in on this mountain.''

''I was afraid of that, dear. You must be going out of your mind with boredom.''

''No, not really,'' Charlene answered.

Zach glanced at her as he put his shirt on, then he grabbed his coat and signaled to her that he was going out. She shook her head no, and pointed to his knee, but he only smiled and slipped out the door.

''The helicopter is free to come for you now,'' her mother was saying.

''Not yet, Mother. It would be dangerous for the pilot.'' There was silence on the other end of the telephone.

''That's very considerate of you, dear, and most unusual for you to be concerned.''

Charlene was trying to see out the window. Where was he going? she wondered. He shouldn't be walking on that leg.

''Are you still there, dear?''

''Yes, Mother. Why don't I call you when the weather gets better,'' she suggested, wanting to end the conversation as quickly as possible.

''That will be fine, dear, if you're certain you're

all right. You sound very strange, or perhaps we have a bad connection."

"I think it's the connection, Mother, and don't worry, I'm fine."

"Is that young man who's your partner treating you any better?"

Charlene had to smile. "Yes, we've worked out our differences."

"I'm pleased to hear that. Well, I won't keep you any longer, dear. I'll wait to hear from you."

"Goodbye, Mother." Charlene hung up the phone and ran for the door. "Zach," she called out. "Damn," she swore softly, realizing he had already disappeared. She stripped off the sheet and quickly began to dress. What was the man doing going out in the deep snow with an injured leg, she fumed as she pulled her boots on, and why had he felt it necessary to leave while she was on the phone? What she had to say to her mother wasn't private.

She couldn't touch him the way she did, couldn't look at him with those green eyes the way she did, if she didn't have feelings for him, he told himself as he leaned against a hitching post and stared off toward the mountains. But having feelings and wanting to spend the rest of your life with someone was a totally different matter.

Silently he cursed Cody Jones for throwing them together. Knowing Charlene Van Payton had changed his life irrevocably. The situation was his own damned fault, he thought despairingly. He'd known from the start it was hopeless. If he'd just stuck to sex and not gotten emotionally involved.

He broke the stick he held and tossed it angrily

aside. Who was he kidding? He was emotionally involved before they'd had sex. He inhaled a deep breath of the clean, cold air, but it did nothing to ease his mounting frustration. He tried to think when she had first gotten such a grip on his emotions. Was it the evening she'd burned the pork chops? No, he smiled to himself, it was when she had been so frightened hearing the wolves howling. Charlene's voice suddenly penetrated his bleak thoughts.

"What are you doing out here, cowboy?" she asked, slipping her arms around his waist.

Automatically his arms went around her and he pressed a kiss on her forehead.

"You are not supposed to be walking on that leg," she scolded.

"It's fine."

"Why did you leave?"

His blue eyes held hers for a long moment. "I thought you needed some privacy, and I needed some fresh air."

"Nothing I had to say to my mother was private." Zach didn't comment, but she was sure she saw a frown cross his face.

"Is Van Payton Enterprises falling apart without you?" he asked, trying to keep the bitterness from his voice.

Charlene laughed. "I'd like to think so, but probably the only person who has realized I'm not there is the cleaning lady who empties my trash can."

Zach smiled at her. "The new Charlene Van Payton will have a different effect on people."

"Do you think so?"

"I know so." He raised her hand and kissed the palm. "I know I'm never going to be the same."

Charlene's eyes searched his face. She wanted him to say more, to tell her what he was feeling, but he didn't.

"Look at that view, Charley," he said, turning her so her back was to him, as he stared at the snow-capped mountain peaks. "Have you ever seen anything like it?"

"No. It's breathtaking," she answered, leaning back against him. "Do you really horseback ride in those mountains?"

"Damned right I do," he said, pulling her closer to him. "It's the only way to go. Wait until you see some of the beautiful lakes around here. Who knows, maybe you'd like to keep a boat here to use when you come in the summer."

Charlene turned in his arms to face him. "Zach," she paused, embarrassed. "I don't know why I told you I enjoyed sailing and golf, because I've never done either," she admitted sheepishly. "Not that I wouldn't like to. I just have never had the opportunity."

Zach smiled tenderly at her. "I didn't think you had, Charley, but I'm glad we cleared that up. I'd hate to go sailing with you if you didn't know what you were doing."

"I wouldn't have let it go that far," she laughed. "When you asked me what I enjoyed doing, I felt embarrassed that I couldn't come up with anything."

"I thought as much."

Charlene laid her head against his chest, thinking he was the most wonderful man in the world. She loved everything about him.

"Is there anything else you want to tell me?" he asked softly, thinking she might be holding back announcing her plans to leave.

Charlene smiled. "I never told you I could play tennis, did I? Because if I did, I can't do that, either."

Zach threw back his head and laughed. "Ah, but you have other talents, sweetheart. Talents far more valuable than being able to play tennis."

"I'm glad you think so," she said, smiling up at him. "I've never been very good at anything."

Her sad smile twisted at Zach's heart. "You've done a lot of things very well since you've been here. You've turned into a good cook, an excellent nursemaid, and the most desirable, exciting woman I've ever had the privilege to know."

"Have you known very many women?" she asked tentatively.

"A few," he answered with a devilish grin.

"Oh, that's right," she said, punching him. "You used to have to beat them off with a stick."

"Used to is the operative phrase," he teased. "Since I've gotten older I don't beat them off any-more. I tell them to come right on."

"Well, let me tell you, Zach Leighton, if I ever catch one of them coming on to you, I'll scratch her eyes out."

"Really, Charley?" he asked, one dark eyebrow raised in skepticism. "I wasn't sure you cared that much."

Charlene stared at him in disbelief. "How could you think that?" she exclaimed. "Do you think I've been making love with you to pass the time?"

He shrugged his shoulders, wondering why he'd started this, but it was too late to turn back now. "I don't know," he answered indolently. "Have you?"

Charlene's eyes filled with tears. "Damn you,

Zach Leighton. How could you say that? I'm not some tramp who falls into bed with just anyone. I . . . I . . ." She couldn't tell him how she really felt, afraid he would laugh at her.

He wanted to pull her into his arms and kiss her senseless. Why the hell had he started this? Was he trying to push her away before she announced that she was leaving? "You what, Charley?" he forced himself to ask.

Charlene stared at him, tears rolling down her face. "I love you," she blurted out before turning and running toward the lodge.

Zach stared after her, but he didn't follow. *So where do we go from here, princess?* he wondered silently. *Is this the beginning or the end for us?* If she went back to San Francisco, would her life change? Would she find some man and settle down with kids, or would she continue to be alone, partying occasionally with her yacht club set? He took a deep breath. She'd find someone, he decided, with a bitter taste in his mouth. One of those idiots she associated with would finally realize that she could be a warm, loving woman.

When Zach entered the lodge he found Charlene sitting on the rug in front of the fireplace, her knees drawn up to her chest. She looked like a little girl with a big problem, he thought as he stared at her for a long moment.

When she chose not to acknowledge his presence, he headed for the kitchen and got two bottles of beer and a glass. When he returned, he sat down on the floor in front of her and poured her beer into the glass, then handed it to her. She glanced up at him, the pain in her green eyes obvious.

"I think we need to talk, Charley."

"You already said enough," she replied petulantly.

"No, I haven't," he said, taking her hand. She tried to pull it away, but he wouldn't let her. "My only excuse is that your mother's phone call rattled me," he admitted. "I've been dreading for the time to come when you could leave, and I figured the time had finally come."

"I didn't think you cared," she said softly, unable to meet his eyes.

"I care too damned much, Charley. Don't you realize that? That's why we're having this problem. How simple it would be if it were just the sex."

Charlene finally looked into his eyes. "You've never said how you felt."

"I thought I had shown you, but I know that's a typical male response," he said with a long sigh. "I love you, honey. I should have told you that before, but I suppose I was afraid to admit it even to myself. Then when you admitted how you really felt about me, it just blew my mind. I've been standing out there in the cold trying to think, and I still don't know how we're going to work this out. You have a very successful life in San Francisco, and my life is here," he said grimly. "And to be honest with you, sweetheart, I won't give up my life on the ranch to live in San Francisco like Cody did. So where does that leave us?"

Charlene fought a new onslaught of tears. She swallowed painfully before answering. "That sounds like an ultimatum."

"I guess it does," he said with a shrug of his shoulders. "But I do have a suggestion," he said, gently touching a tear that ran down her cheek.

"What is that?"

"Let's not think about this situation now. I don't see any way we're going to come up with an instant solution. We'll enjoy our time together, and when you can get off this mountain, we'll discuss it again. You and I both know the problem isn't going to go away."

"Do you really think we can pretend it doesn't exist?" Charlene asked.

"We can give it a try, sweetheart. Otherwise we're going to make ourselves miserable worrying about it, and we'll probably end up resenting each other."

Charlene sniffed. "I believe this is what's called the Scarlett O'Hara solution. We'll think about it tomorrow."

"Something like that," he said, pulling her into his arms.

NINETEEN

They both agreed not to think about their future, but for the next couple of weeks, it was never far from either of their minds, causing tempers to be on edge. Fortunately the arguments were always minor, and they were intelligent enough to realize the tension was getting to them. In the meantime, they tried to keep busy making plans for changes at the ranch, snowmobiling in the beautiful countryside, and making slow, passionate love as if each time was their last.

"This is my favorite time of day," Charlene sighed as they stood on the deck and watched the sun go down. Zach had his arms around her, keeping her warm and cherished against his strong body. "The light at this time does magical things to the mountains."

" 'Let me walk in beauty, and make my eyes ever behold the red and purple sunset,' " he quoted.

"That's beautiful," Charlene exclaimed. "Did you just make it up?"

"No. It comes from an Indian prayer," he said, kissing her on the temple. "There have been times when I've stood here staring at those mountains and was sure I could see the ghosts of all those who have come and gone over them; the Indians, prospectors, and explorers. I mentioned that to Cody one time and he told me they were phantoms at dusk. He claimed that everyone who loves the Tetons sees them sooner or later."

Charlene smiled. "When I arrived here I thought anyone who preferred this kind of life had to be out of their mind. Now I can understand it. The sense of remoteness one feels here makes all the problems of the world seem so far away."

Zach sighed, wishing that were true. "Yet they always seem to manage to invade our thoughts, don't they?"

"Yes," she answered softly. "Do you know, I used to lie in bed alone and listen to tapes of the ocean, or birds singing, or sounds of the forests, never thinking to take the time to enjoy the real thing. Now here I stand, a part of nature in this magnificent place that's both serene and savage."

His warm laughter surrounded her. "You're not alone, sweetheart. I read somewhere that the average American spends eighty-four percent of his life indoors. That means that they miss all this. They live in a world of wall-to-wall carpet, air conditioning, and pollution."

"Watch it, Leighton, you're describing my world."

Zach gritted his teeth. That wasn't what he wanted to hear. He wanted her to consider this her world, to consider him her life. Didn't she realize he wanted to share a home, have children, and spend the rest of his life with her? If she decided to go back to San Francisco to pick up her life would he be able to stand firm on his decision not to leave the ranch, or would he follow after her and try to make a go of it in the city? The very thought made his breath catch. He had already tried city life and had hated it. He truly doubted even Charlene's love could make it tolerable, and then he'd be in the same situation Cody had found himself in; a wife, a child, and a life he couldn't stand.

"Zach, do you realize it hasn't snowed once the past two weeks?" she commented, interrupting his thoughts.

"I know. It's most unusual."

She didn't tell him she had been hoping for a blizzard because she wasn't ready to face their problem yet. "What do you want to do this evening?" she asked.

Zach laughed deep in his chest before whispering explicitly erotic things in her ear that he wanted to do to her.

"People don't do that," she exclaimed.

"Oh yes, they do, sweetheart," he laughed, "and I'll be glad to show you why they do it."

"Gee," she said, a teasing smile on her beautiful face. "I was thinking more on the lines of a pool game."

Zach threw back his head and laughed. "We haven't gotten around to that yet, have we? Well, since I'm still full from your wonderful meatloaf, maybe we should play pool for a while. It won't take me long to teach you, and then,'' he said, twisting an imaginary mustache, "I get to do what I want."

"I've spoiled you, Zach Leighton. I'm going to have to stop letting you have your way all the time."

Zach started to retort that if that were true, she wouldn't consider going back to San Francisco, but he didn't. "I think we should place a wager on the game," he suggested.

Charlene smiled to herself. "And what do you suggest we wager?"

"Something very valuable."

Charlene stared at him. "Are you referring to my half of the ranch again?" she asked suspiciously.

"No, sweetheart, I was referring to your body and soul."

Tears gathered in Charlene's eyes. "Don't you know you already own my body and soul?"

"Do I?" was all he said as they headed back inside. What the hell was wrong with him? he wondered. He felt edgy and restless. "Why don't you put on some music, while I build a fire in the game room," he suggested, trying to shake the feeling.

"Would you like a cup of hot chocolate?" she asked.

"Sounds good, but don't forget the ice cream on top," he said, smacking her on the bottom as she headed toward the kitchen.

Charlene hummed as she heated the milk. Even a simple act like preparing hot chocolate seemed a pleasure when she was with Zach. Why then couldn't she just commit herself to him? She knew he wouldn't go to San Francisco and live her way of life, and she really wasn't sure that was what she wanted anyway. She wouldn't be able to stand seeing him miserable living in the city. Yet where did that leave them? Could she possibly adapt to his world?

She closed her eyes and sighed. Her mother and father had tried to bring these two worlds together and had failed miserably, nearly ruining three lives in the bargain. "Oh, Cody," she whispered softly. "You brought Zach and me together. Tell me what to do. Am I repeating the same mistake with the same sad ending?"

"Hey, where's that hot chocolate?" Zach shouted from the game room.

"Coming right up."

"The fire is blazing, so I'll put the music on. How about some Garth Brooks?"

"Is that the one about friends in low places?" she asked as she joined him.

"That's the one. Is that how you think of our relationship, Charley? Am I your friend from the other side of the tracks?" he asked with a smile, yet there was a tinge of bitterness in his voice. "If you'd met me in San Francisco, you would probably have turned your nose up at me."

Charlene wrapped her arms around his neck. "I might have, cowboy," she teased, "but I doubt it. I think you would have made an impression on me no matter where we met."

"Is that right, Charley?" he asked, one dark eyebrow raised in skepticism. "Even among all your rich pretty boys at the yacht club?"

"Particularly among the rich pretty boys," she assured him, a smile on her face.

Seeing amusement in her eyes made him irrationally angry. "I'm not in the mood for your teasing,

Charley," he said, moving to stand before the fireplace.

Charlene followed him, wrapping her arms around him. "I wasn't teasing, Zach. Why would you think so? You know how I feel about you."

"Yeah, but how long will that last? Until you can get off this mountain?" he asked bitterly.

"Zach, please let's not start arguing again."

Zach stared down into her green eyes for a long moment, then he folded her into his arms and held her tight against his chest. "I'm sorry," he whispered. "I don't know what's wrong with me. I have this feeling of impending doom, and it scares the hell out of me."

She ran her hand through his thick wavy hair in a loving gesture. "It's the tension, Zach. It's been so thick between us for the past couple of weeks that it cracks in the air. Our resolve not to think about the future has only made it worse."

Zach laughed caustically. "You're dealing with a man who never does anything halfway. When I make a mistake, sweetheart, I do it wholeheartedly. I suppose we would have been better off to sit down that night and discuss our problems, but truthfully I was afraid the outcome would ruin what we had, even if what we had was only temporary."

"We will work something out, love," she asserted, pulling his head down to meet his lips.

"Charley," he whispered against her lips. "I want to love you."

"Will that make your melancholy mood go away?" she asked, placing kisses along his neck.

He picked her up and headed toward the bed. "It's worth a try."

"What about our pool game?"

"It will have to wait," he said, laying her on the bed. He began to unbutton her shirt, kissing her warm flesh as he slowly slipped it off. "You are so beautiful, and so damned desirable. I want to savor your sweetness, every inch of your sweetness," he whispered as he undid her jeans and leisurely slid them down over her hips, his lips following the path.

Charlene's breath caught as his tongue moved down her side and across her stomach. She arched her hips, moaning as the fire began to build. He hadn't touched her with his hands, and her breasts and between her thighs ached for his touch, yet he seemed content to torture her with his tongue. She felt as if she were being drawn into him, body and soul.

"Zach, please," she moaned, wrapping her hand in his thick hair.

"Please what, love?" he asked, coming back to her mouth.

"Touch me," she begged. "Kiss me . . ."

His tongue plundered her mouth and she matched his passion with her own, rubbing her body against his. "No," she protested as his lips left her mouth and began a slow, burning trail down her stomach. "I want you in me, please, Zach, come to me," she begged as her hands moved seductively over his hard-muscled body.

"Not yet," he whispered, his voice husky with desire. He flicked his tongue around the nipple of each breast, then moved lower over her satiny skin until he was inches away from the apex of her womanhood. His tongue burned a trail down her thigh, and then slowly back up. She trembled beneath the onslaught, but her movements had ceased. She didn't dare move, afraid she would lose the incredible sensations he was evoking. Her heart hammered against her chest as she felt him gently part her thighs. As soon as she felt his feather-light touch, wave after wave of rapture washed over her. She cried out her pleasure, her nails digging into his shoulders.

Moments later, he lifted her hips to meet his pulsating length. Her emotions were spinning as he drove into her welcoming softness.

They both lay exhausted, their breaths mingling as Zach held her tightly against him. He kissed the sweet silkiness of her hair, thinking he could never let her go.

Charlene's passion-filled eyes met his. "I love you," she whispered.

He kissed her gently. "I love you, too, sweetheart." He was about to tell her he wanted it to be like this forever, when the phone rang.

"Don't answer it," she suggested, but he rolled over and sat up on the side of the bed. "Your mother has perfect timing."

"What makes you think it's my mother?" she asked defensively as she sat up and slipped into her shirt.

"Answer the damned phone," he said as he pulled on his pants. "She's probably heard that we haven't had any snow up here for the past two weeks and there isn't any reason you can't get off the mountain. Who the hell knows what she wants, but you can bet it isn't good news."

"Stop being a grouch," she said, sticking her tongue out at him as she picked up the phone. "Hello."

There was silence for a long moment, then a female voice asked, "Who is this?"

Charlene felt an unexplainable rush of irritation. "Who did you wish to speak to?" she asked tersely.

"Zach Leighton," the woman answered.

Charlene held the phone out to him. "It's for you."

She turned her back to him and slowly buttoned her shirt. From the cryptic, one-sided conversation she was hearing, she knew the woman was someone Zach had been seeing. When she heard him tell the woman it was his partner who had answered the phone, she saw red, but the crowning blow came when she heard him tell the woman it wasn't a good time for her to come for a visit, that the weather was still too bad. Her heart was pounding and she actually felt sick to her stomach, she was so angry and hurt.

"Hello . . . hello, are you there, Tess? I'll be damned," he swore as he hung the phone up. "The line went dead."

"How terrible for you," Charlene said, each word ringing with bitter fury. "Then you didn't have a chance to tell her I'd be out of here soon and she should come then."

"For God's sake, Charley, what are you talking about?"

"Your partner!" she screamed. "That's what you said I was." She laughed bitterly. "All this time I thought I meant something to you, but I heard you tell her I was *just* your partner."

"Damnit, Charley, you're blowing this all out of proportion. Tess is just a friend . . ."

"You didn't have to turn her away on my account.

I could have taken a walk while you two do whatever you do,'' she screamed, tears running down her face. ''I certainly wouldn't want to be in the way.''

Zach stared at her, his eyes narrowed angrily. ''I've done nothing wrong,'' he hissed, grabbing her by the shoulders and forcing her to face him. ''Now I want you to stop this tirade, Charley. It's ludicrous. Tess is just a friend. She knows how boring it gets being up here on the mountain alone, and when the weather breaks she usually tries to come up and bring me . . .''

Before he could finish she jerked away from him. ''She comes up to the ranch and provides you with sex, but since I'm here to do that, you don't need her right now, is that it?'' she continued relentlessly. ''You told me once that for a relationship to work there had to be truth and honesty. Why don't you practice what you preach, Zach Leighton? You're a hypocrite and a liar, just like I thought in the beginning, and I hate you!''

He grabbed her and held her tightly by the arms, his fingers digging into her soft flesh. ''And you've reverted back into the bitch you were when you arrived here,'' he said between gritted teeth. ''If you're looking for an excuse to bow out of this relationship, you've got it. I don't need this abuse. But before we sever our connection, you're going to listen to me,'' he said, giving her a firm shake.

''I don't want to hear anything you have to say,'' she cried brokenly. ''Now let me go.''

''Not until you hear me out. I started to tell you that Tess is the sister of a good friend who runs the art gallery in town. When the weather breaks, *they* drive up together to bring me fresh vegetables and fruit, and to take back any paintings that I want to sell. I told her not to come at this time because I didn't want to have to share our time with anyone."

Charlene stared at him, distress written all over her face. "They come together?" she managed to get out between sobs.

"That's right, sweetheart," he drawled sarcastically as he shoved her away from him. "Now you can leave any damned time you want to. There's nothing holding you here."

He grabbed his coat off the hook and headed for the door while she stood frozen to the spot, her whole world falling apart. When he slammed the door, she collapsed on the bed, sobbing her heart out.

TWENTY

Zach walked until he felt numb from the cold, but it hadn't helped this time. He still felt as hopeless and desolate as when he'd left the lodge, even though his anger had evaporated. He turned around and headed back, disgusted with himself for being such a fool. The situation had been impossible from the start. Why hadn't he realized that instead of falling head over heels in love with the girl?

He hesitated at the door of the lodge, wondering what he was going to say to Charley, or if he should say anything at all. *Let her go,* he told himself. *You'll save yourself a hell of a lot of pain if you just let it end now.*

Slowly he opened the door. The fire had died down and the room felt cold. He glanced around, wondering where she'd gone when he noticed her lying curled up on the bed, her knees drawn up like a little child. Her face was pale, and her cheeks were stained with tears.

"Oh, God, Charley," he moaned, feeling his own emotions welling up inside. "What the hell are we going to do? How can I just forget that I love you more than life itself?" He gently sat down on the side of the bed.

When Charlene felt the movement she instantly sat up, staring at him, her sea-green eyes red and swollen. "I was so afraid," she whispered. "I didn't think you were going to come back."

Zach pulled her into his arms and held her. "Where would I go, Charley?"

"I don't know," she whispered, clinging to him. "I'm so sorry, Zach. I don't know what got into me."

"The same thing that got into me," he said, stroking her hair. "It's called fear. It makes people do strange things. We knew when we started this relationship that it wasn't going to be easy, but I don't think either of us knew it would be impossible. We can't go back, but we can't seem to go forward, either."

"You're wrong, Zach," she said, sitting up to look him in the eyes. "I decided while you were gone that I wanted to stay here with you."

Zach laughed bitterly. "Too little too late, Charley. A decision like that can't be made to pacify me because we had an argument. You'd end up regretting it, I'd end up hating you for it, and both of our lives would be miserable. We've been dealt these cards, Charley, and now we're going to have to play with them. My life is here and your life is in San Francisco."

The color drained from her face. "No. I won't accept that," she replied vehemently. "I agree, maybe we need time to work things out, but I refuse to believe we can't do that."

Zach smiled patiently. "You were a cynic when you arrived here, princess, and now you're a dreamer. I'm not sure which is worse. Be honest with yourself. Do you really think you could spend the rest of your life on this ranch, isolated in the winter and playing hostess to a bunch of greenhorns pretending to be cowboys in the summer? During the peak season there's never a spare minute to sit and relax. Someone is always demanding something from you. It's a hard life at best, Charley. We don't have a yacht club, or fancy department stores, or exclusive restaurants."

Charlene stared at him, her eyes haunted and filled with pain. "You don't want me to stay, do you?"

His chest constricted at the look on her face. He should tell her that he didn't want her to stay. It would be easier on both of them in the long run, but he couldn't cause her more pain. "Lie down and let me hold you, Charley. You look exhausted."

"You didn't answer my question, Zach. Do you want me to go?"

His fingers lightly brushed her cheek. "What I want doesn't really matter, love."

"Do you want me to go?" she persisted.

Zach sighed as he pulled her back into his arms. "It's the last thing I want, Charley, but it doesn't make a damned bit of difference what I want. You and I both know it won't work. Your father and mother proved that."

"The risks of failing may be incredibly high, but nothing is worth having if you don't have to work at it."

Zach smiled. "Is this the same Charlene Van Payton who arrived on my doorstep a couple of months ago?"

"No. It's a very different Charlene Van Payton. That's what I've been trying to tell you. I'm not afraid to give this life a chance, Zach. You're more of a coward than I am. You won't even consider a change. Admit it, the fact that I have money eats at you, at your damn male pride."

"You have a point, Charley. I do feel the man should be able to take care of his wife and children, and I'm smart enough to know that I can never provide you with the way of life that you're accustomed to, and I sure as hell am not going to let you keep me, or provide me with menial jobs to keep me busy while you run your empire."

"I wouldn't do that and you know it," she said in frustration, "and I don't need to be kept in luxury, Zach. All I need is a home and a man to love me. And if being successful is what you're worried about, you could open an art gallery in San Francisco and be very successful, or you could become involved in environmental issues in San Francisco."

Zach smiled tenderly. "I've considered it, Charley, but I'm honest enough to know it wouldn't work. This is my home. This is where I want to raise a family. I never led you to believe anything else."

"No, you didn't, but that was before you told me you loved me," she whispered.

"Sweetheart, it's late," he said, rubbing his thumb along her jawline. "Arguing about this now isn't doing either of us any good. I'm so tired I can't even think straight. Lie down and let me hold you. We'll talk in the morning."

Exhausted, Charlene cuddled up against him, savoring the feel of his arms around her. He lifted her chin and gently kissed her, then drew the quilt up over them. They both quickly fell into a restless, uneasy sleep.

Charlene turned over and pulled the pillow over her head, trying to block out the obnoxious noise that rumbled through her head. Suddenly she threw the pillow aside and sat up, realizing it was the sound of a helicopter hovering over the lodge.

"Good morning, princess," Zach said from the bathroom doorway. "It seems your transportation has arrived. I'll put on a pot of coffee while you get packed. I imagine your pilot will appreciate a cup of coffee if he finds a place to set down."

Charlene stared after him, still unable to fathom what was actually happening. Why would her mother have sent the helicopter without telling her first? She told her that she would call her when she was ready, and she wasn't ready to return to San Francisco or the intrusion of the outside world. They hadn't had a chance to work things out.

She leaped from the bed and began to dress, determined to make Zach admit he didn't want her to go. The noise was terrible for another few minutes, then finally the engine stopped and she could hear the whirling blades as they slowly came to a stop.

"You want to invite your pilot in," Zach shouted from the kitchen as if this were just a visitor paying a social call. "Maybe he'll want some breakfast."

"No," she said firmly as she stood in the kitchen doorway. "I want to talk to you. The time has come for us to make a decision," she persisted.

"Will you get some sugar from the pantry?" he said nonchalantly, his back to her.

"Zach. For God's sake, will you listen to me? I love you. I don't want to leave you."

He turned around and looked at her. "Let's face it, Charley, fate must be intervening, because I wouldn't have given that pilot a snowball's chance in hell to land that thing on this mountain, but he did it. Now it's time for you to pack and go home. It will give both of us time to think."

"Go with me, Zach," she pleaded. "At least see San Francisco. Haven't you been isolated up here long enough?"

He smiled at her patiently. "I can't leave here, Charley, even if I wanted to. You forget, I have our investment to protect. I'm going to take a walk while you pack. I'll tell your pilot there's coffee on."

"Zach, please don't leave like this," she begged, knowing he wouldn't come back until she was gone. "I can't bear it."

He laughed bitterly. "I can't stand out front and wave goodbye, if that's what you want, sweetheart."

"That isn't what I want and you know it," she said as tears ran down her face.

"You'll be fine, Charley." He gazed down at her, studying her face as if trying to memorize every feature. "Just take care of yourself," he said brokenly before capturing her mouth in a deep kiss. When it ended, he grabbed his jacket and left the kitchen without another word.

TWENTY-ONE

FOUR MONTHS LATER

Charlene kept busy during the days and evenings, giving her financial support and time to environmental groups, organizing the workers at Van Payton Enterprises to be environmentally aware, and taking care of her usual duties. She could almost forget her loneliness while tirelessly working, because she was doing something worthwhile—but the nights were a different story. The nights were so painfully lonely. She had attempted to rejoin the circle of friends she had, but they all seemed so dull and shallow. The parties and carousing no longer held an appeal for her. Instead, she thought about the evenings standing on the deck of the lodge and looking off at the mountains with Zach's arms around her, or sitting in front of the fire, cuddled up in his arms. She ached for his touch, for his companionship.

The pencil she was twisting in her hand suddenly snapped. "Damn," she whispered, tossing it on the desk. She was wound tighter than a drum. She closed her eyes and leaned her head back against the chair. She could almost see him, laughter shining in his sky-blue eyes. As she remembered a snow fight they had, a fleeting smile crossed her face. He had rubbed snow all down her shirt, and it had finally ended up with him carrying her inside and making slow, passionate love to her.

"Charlene, are you all right?" her mother interrupted her thoughts, alarmed at the dark circles under her eyes.

Charlene opened her eyes and found Emily standing in the doorway. "I'm fine," she answered, moving papers around on her desk.

"It's no wonder you are exhausted, dear. You can't keep up this pace of working all day and then spend your evenings doing volunteer work."

"It's something I need to do, Mother."

Emily sat down in the chair across from her daughter. "I realize that, dear, and I must admit, I'm extremely proud of you for the worthwhile work you're doing, but I think what you really need to do is make peace with your partner."

Charlene's eyes widened in disbelief. "I don't know what you're talking about."

"Of course you do, dear. Don't you think I can see the pain in your eyes? Most of the time we're alone, you're staring off into space, thinking about him. All I can say is he must be a remarkable young man to have changed you the way he did. No one has mentioned it to me directly, but I've heard people talking about how pleasant and gracious you've become."

Charlene smiled. "Zach taught me to feel good

about myself, Mother, and he showed me what is important in life."

"Then why didn't you just send the helicopter back and stay with him? The only reason I sent it was because the phones were dead and I was concerned for you."

"I know, Mother. You already explained that, but I suppose now that I think about it, it was time to come home. The last week I was there, all we did was argue."

Emily looked concerned. "Then this young man didn't return your love?"

Charlene laughed bitterly. "Oh, he loved me, Mother, but not enough to come back to San Francisco with me. He said Cody had tried it and failed, and he was smart enough to know that it wouldn't work for him, either.

Emily closed her eyes, trying to gather her thoughts. This situation was forcing her to watch her own life being played before her eyes once again.

"I am so sorry, darling," Emily sighed.

"For what, Mother?"

"For depriving you of your father. I realized a long time ago that I would have been much happier if I had gone to Wyoming with Cody," she admitted. "We would have made friends together, raised a family together. Instead, I tried to impose my friends on him, and when he felt out of place I couldn't imagine why. I couldn't see that my friends weren't accepting him. I thought the solution was to have your grandmother give him a position in the company so he'd feel as if he had something worthwhile to do, but the position she chose to give him made him the laughingstock of the company, and I didn't see that, either. Every mistake that was made in our marriage was mine, Charlene. Now I see you making the same mistakes, and it breaks my heart. If you love this young man, do something about it. Don't end up like me, wishing you could turn back the hands of time.''

Charlene shook her head, fighting back tears for herself and her mother. ''I already told him I wanted to stay with him, Mother, but he wouldn't let me. He said our relationship had been doomed from the beginning. Does that sound like a man in love?'' she asked caustically.

''And you're going to accept that?''

''Yes,'' she said as she stood up and walked toward the windows. ''I have no choice. Zach made it very clear how he wanted it. I've accepted the fact that it wasn't meant to be, and this morning I decided that it would be best to relinquish my half of the ranch to him. That way maybe I can put him out of my mind altogether, and get on with my life.''

Emily moved to stand behind her daughter. ''Are you sure that's really what you want to do?''

''It's the only chance I have of putting him out of my mind,'' she whispered.

''All right, dear. Then let me handle the details. When the deed has been cleared and given to him, I'll let you know.''

Charlene wiped a tear from her cheek as she turned around. ''Thank you, Mother. I appreciate that.''

Emily hugged her daughter. ''Don't worry about a thing, dear. I'll take care of everything.''

An unusually mild winter allowed Zach to start preparing for the tourist season in mid-February. He threw himself into building the fire pit in the deck, but it made him think of Charley. He ordered a hot tub to be delivered in March, and it made him think of Charley. When he went through the cabins, checking on the pipes, he thought how drab everything looked, and remembered that Charley was going to redecorate.

"Damn it to hell," he swore. "Why can't I put her out of my mind? She was spoiled and pampered, a rich brat who always got what she wanted. Why in the world would I want to spend my life with someone like that?"

Zach leaned over and picked up his hammer. "You're going to drive yourself crazy, Leighton. You haven't heard a thing from her in three months. She could have at least called."

He stared off at the snowcapped mountains. *You didn't give her much reason to call, you fool,* he concluded. *I'd say you made it perfectly clear that the relationship was over. Wasn't that the way you wanted it?*

"I didn't expect her to haunt my days and nights," he said aloud.

The sound of a motor straining to get up the mountain broke into his bleak thoughts. He was expecting lumber to be delivered for fence repairs, so he headed toward the drive to wait.

"Howdy, Zach," Will Standard, the owner of the lumber yard greeted. "I hope I have everything you need. That's one hell of a climb with a loaded truck."

Zach smiled at the man who said the same thing every time he came up the mountain. "At least the weather is good,'' Zach said as he pulled on his leather gloves to help unload the truck.

It took about thirty minutes to unload, wood, nails, paint, and some bricks to line his fire pit. ''Why don't you come in and have a cup of coffee?'' Zach invited.

''Thanks, but I better get back down the mountain. I promised the kids I'd take them to look for a horse this afternoon.''

''Well, thanks for delivering this stuff. I'll see you soon.''

Zach had started toward the lodge when Will called him back. ''I almost forgot,'' he said, waving an envelope. ''Lily gave me this letter for you. She said it looked important and she didn't want it to sit around until you came to town.''

As he noticed the San Francisco postmark, Zach's heart skipped a beat. ''Thanks, Will. Tell Lily I appreciate it.''

He headed toward the lodge, staring at the letter. It was typed. Would Charlene type him a letter? It didn't seem very personal, but hell, he'd take a typewritten letter from her. Sitting on one of the benches on the deck, he continued to stare at the letter as if he expected it to speak to him. ''Open it, fool. You're not going to know what it is until you do.''

Slowly Zach opened the envelope. Immediately his eyes went to Emily Van Payton's signature and he felt a dull ache all over. He read it once, then again, and by the second time, rage exploded in his brain and he threw the letter aside and began to pace the deck. ''So Charley has decided she doesn't want to be my partner and wants to sell me her share for a reasonable amount. I wonder just what the hell she considers reasonable,'' he fumed. It didn't matter, he told himself. If she didn't want to be his partner, he'd find some way to buy her out. Hell, he'd mortgage everything he owned to put her out of his life.

He leaned over and picked the letter up, reading it for a third time. It stipulated that he had to be in San Francisco at two o'clock on March 29th. Leave it to Charley to make it easy on herself.

TWENTY-TWO

Charlene entered her mother's office, expecting to have lunch with her as they had been doing for the past several months. "Good afternoon. You got away from the house early this morning," she commented as she poured herself a cup of coffee.

"Yes. I had some important business to take care of," Emily explained. "You're looking lovely today, dear. I'm glad you chose that outfit."

Charlene glanced down at her clothing. "Why?" she asked as she picked up a roll and spread mayonnaise on it.

"We have an important meeting at two today."

"Oh, really? Is it with the Schuler group about the Arizona property?"

"No, dear," Emily said, studying her daughter's face. "It's with Zach Leighton about the Wyoming property."

Charlene sat down in the chair as if her legs had been knocked out from beneath her. "Mother . . .

you said you'd take care of this,'' she protested as her heart pounded erratically in her chest. ''I don't want to see him. I *can't* see him!''

''I'm sorry, dear, but according to Jeremy, that isn't legally possible. Now, if you had wanted to sell him your share it would have been different, but since you've chosen to turn it over to him gratis, signatures and witnesses are needed.''

''Oh, God,'' Charlene moaned, rubbing her temples. What was she going to do? She couldn't face him. The pain had finally begun to ease, and now it was all going to come rushing back. ''Isn't there any other way?''

''I'm sorry, dear,'' Emily said, patting her daughter's shoulder, ''but perhaps this is best. If you face the man here on your territory, you'll realize he'd never fit in, and then you'll be able to put him out of your mind.'' She smiled at the confused look on her daughter's face. ''That *is* what you want to do, isn't it?''

''Of course,'' Charlene said with little enthusiasm. ''What time is it now?'' shc asked, not bothering to look at her own watch.

''It's one-fifteen, dear. We have plenty of time to enjoy our lunch.''

Charlene stared at the half-made sandwich, thinking if she tried to take a bite she'd surely choke on it. She wanted to run, to hide, anything but come face-to-face with Zach Leighton.

''You're a Van Payton, my dear, you can handle this. Show the man what a fool he was to let you go,'' Emily said calculatingly. Charlene nibbled on one nail, considering what her mother had said.

Maybe facing him would exorcise him from her mind. "What time did you say it was?"

Emily smiled. "One-seventeen, dear."

Charlene stood on wobbly legs. "I'm going to freshen up," she said, taking a deep, steadying breath. "I assume this meeting is in the boardroom."

"That's right. It will just be you and Mr. Leighton, and Jeremy and myself."

"Fine. I'll see you there," Charlene said, before heading back to her own office.

At two o'clock Charlene stood staring out the window of the boardroom. This wasn't going to be easy, but it was the best way, she told herself. She would face him, cool, calm, and collected, sign the ranch over to him, then get on with her life. That was all there was to it. He was coming to her environment, and she'd show him that his rejection hadn't touched her life.

She glanced at her watch. It was now five after two. Maybe he wasn't coming, she thought hopefully. Then the door opened and Jeremy entered, leading Zach Leighton into the office.

Their eyes met and her heart stopped, she was sure of it. He was dressed in a black Western-style suit and a white shirt, and she thought she'd never seen anyone so sinfully handsome. How could she ever have thought this meeting would exorcise him from her mind? She wanted to rush into his arms.

The moment was shattered when she realized her mother was shaking his hand and thanking him for coming. *Be cool, calm, and collected,* she told herself. *Cool, calm, and collected,* she repeated over and over.

"How nice to see you, Zach," she greeted, offering her hand to him.

Her eyes widened as his touch seemed to sear her. She stumbled over a few inane comments, then directed him to take a seat across from her.

Zach couldn't take his eyes off her. He'd actually found himself speechless when their eyes met, his anger and irritation at being summoned to San Francisco quickly disappearing.

After polite requests were made about coffee or tea, the lawyer began to read the papers in front of him. Zach only half listened, the negotiations suddenly unimportant. He wondered what she had on beneath the stylish sea-green suit that matched her eyes perfectly. It sure as hell wasn't red flannel underwear, he thought, a devilish gleam in his eyes.

He looks so pleased with himself, Charlene thought. *I suppose he thinks he's won. I hope you never forget our nights together, Zach Leighton,* she thought silently. *I hope every time you're with a woman, I invade your thoughts.*

He was stunned by how much he wanted the cool, sophisticated woman sitting across from him. They had nothing in common, he told himself. Look at her sitting there so calm and unaffected. She fit into the boardroom scene as if she'd been born to it. Hell, she had been born to it, he reminded himself. *Keep your guard up, Leighton. She's up to something. You were a fool to think it could be any different.*

Charlene stared back at the man across from her. His eyes were bluer than she remembered, and his hair had been trimmed to a respectable length, though she preferred it longer. God, she had forgotten how wide his shoulders were. She swallowed with difficulty, remembering how hard and muscular his body was when he was naked, and what those large, calloused hands could do to *her* body.

"And so, Mr. Leighton, Ms. Van Payton has decided to relinquish her holdings in Hawk's Cry Ranch to you."

Zach tore his eyes away from Charlene's face. "I'm sorry, what did you say?"

"I said, Ms. Van Payton has decided to . . ."

"No!" Charlene shouted, suddenly on her feet. Everyone stared at her. "I mean, I want to discuss this with Mr. Leighton before I make my final decision."

Here it comes, Zach thought. *She's going to try to take me for every cent I have. I almost lost it there for a moment. I actually thought I heard the lawyer say she was relinquishing her share to me.*

"Ms. Van Payton, I don't think that is a good idea," her lawyer warned. "As you know, I haven't agreed with your decision, and there could be legal problems . . ."

"Let them discuss it alone, Jeremy," Emily said, getting to her feet.

"No, stay where you are," Charlene gently ordered. "There isn't any reason you can't hear what I have to say."

Zach stared at her, his eyes becoming hard with suspicion. He shouldn't have come, he told himself. By God, he'd almost decided to make a try of it in San Francisco. He should have known she'd pull something, but what the hell was she up to?

"I have decided to return to Jackson Hole and run the Hawk's Cry Ranch with Mr. Leighton," she announced, staring into his unreadable eyes. "I think the ranch could use a woman's touch. Is that agreeable to you, Mr. Leighton?''

It took a long moment for a smile to come over Zach's face. "That's very agreeable, Ms. Van Payton, as long as you agree to become my wife. I don't think we should continue to live in sin.''

"Zach,'' she exclaimed, glancing toward her mother. She was amazed to find her smiling.

"Well, Charley?'' Zach asked, getting to his feet. "Is that agreeable to you?''

Charlene smiled. "That is very agreeable, Mr. Leighton.''

"Wonderful,'' Emily said, clapping her hands. "I was wondering how long it was going to take you two to come to your senses. You will never know how worried I've been that you would make the same mistake I made,'' she said, hugging her daughter.

"Thank you, Mother,'' Charlene whispered.

When Charlene and Zach were alone, they finally moved into each other's arms. "God, how I've missed you, Charley,'' he swore, placing kisses all over her face.

"I thought when you didn't call that you were probably glad to be rid of me,'' she admitted hesitantly.

He touched his warm fingers to her lips, silencing her. "Every minute of every day I've thought about you. I kept telling myself that we had no common ground to build a relationship on, but then I realized we had the most important thing: love. I love you, Charley. My life is meaningless without you. I spent yesterday evening checking out art studios along the bay, and I think I found one . . .''

"No,'' she said, this time silencing him with her

lips. "Knowing that you are willing to come here for me means more to me than you'll ever know, but that isn't what I want, Zach. I've missed the ranch terribly. I want us to go back there and live happily ever after with a bunch of kids."

He moved her away at arm's length. "I'm not going to have you making the only concession, Charley. What if we spend the winters here in San Francisco?"

Charlene smiled through her tears. "I don't know about you, cowboy, but I'm sure the winter is going to be my favorite time at the ranch. Just you and me making love."

Zach smiled. "Well, maybe I can force myself to live with you making all the sacrifices . . ."

Her tears tasted warm and salty on his lips as he kissed her, long and deep. "Are you afraid, Charley?" he asked tenderly as he held her face between his hands.

She smiled through her tears. "The only thing I'm afraid of is that you'll be upset when you hear my plans for the ranch."

"What kind of plans?" he asked suspiciously.

"I insist on having our own private hot tub." She smiled seductively.

"It's already been installed," he announced with a mischievous grin, "but until we get back to the ranch, I just happen to have a Jacuzzi in my hotel room. What do you think?"

"I think I can hardly wait," she said, her mouth grazing his in a promising kiss. "Let's go make a baby, Zach."

He grabbed her hand and led her toward the door. "Your wish is my command, sweetheart."

wall. "Knowing that you are willing to come here [illegible] makes me [illegible] than you'll [illegible] what I want [illegible]" He rubbed the [illegible] there and live [illegible]

[illegible]

Carlotta smiled [illegible] "I don't know [illegible] who's going to laugh [illegible] if you and [illegible]

Zachariah [illegible] "Well, maybe [illegible] myself to [illegible] all the [illegible]"

[illegible] as he [illegible] and [illegible] "I may [illegible]" he [illegible] between his hands.

[illegible] "The only thing I'm afraid of is that [illegible] you wear [illegible]"

"What kind of [illegible]" she asked [illegible]

"[illegible]" She [illegible]

"It's already been [illegible]" [illegible] get back to the [illegible]

"I think I [illegible] why," she said, her [illegible]

He [illegible] her [illegible] and [illegible] her toward the [illegible]

[illegible]

SHARE THE FUN . . .
SHARE YOUR NEW-FOUND TREASURE!!